STEELEYE: THE W

'Prepare for your death Steeleye, life and good fortune have evaded you this never-day.' Yellow spoke the words like a lord and master exacting punishment on a wayward servant, but even Yellow knew nothing of the fearless power that lay dormant in the body of the Eumigs' creation.

Steeleye let fly a blast from his eye and shivered the length of the Codas before him, heating their body of metal, throwing in his own test of strength; a simple gesture to show his quarry that they would best prepare more carefully the death strike they wished to inflict.

The Codas snatched at Steeleye, overreaching to a metre behind him, overbalancing and waivering the full length of their steely tension. Steeleye blasted again at the weakest point of the arm, projecting through twenty metres beside him. The length snapped and one part fell, scattering its million components like black pins. The move gave him no advantage, for the severed part reassembled into a spearhead and took on a separate life, launching an attack from flank and front. Steeleye jumped, lifting his agile body ten metres into the air and over the back section that now spread like a dreadful contagion about his feet.

Also by the same author,
and available in Coronet Books:

The Coming of Steeleye

Steeleye: The Wideways

Saul Dunn

CORONET BOOKS
Hodder and Stoughton, London

First published in Great Britain in 1976 by Coronet Books

The characters and situations in this book are entirely imaginary and bear no relation to any real person or actual happening

Printed and bound in Great Britain
for Coronet Books
Hodder and Stoughton, London
By C. Nicholls & Company Ltd.
The Philips Park Press, Manchester

ISBN 0 340 20740 6

"To those who can 'see', the Universe is like a pin-ball machine, each move of the ball quite logical, confined within the territories of action and reaction. The ball can be bounced back and forth as long as the player has skill enough to keep it going. But eventually something will alter, and it will sink to the bottom. Some players are skilled, some lucky, but most simply play a game."

The Biographies of Steeleye. Haephranis. UA ref 467/df/s

Chapter 1

The young man moved restlessly in his sleep, the blinds at the window flapped, rain spattered in, blown onto the bed-room floor. He shifted his agitated body yet again, thrown into this confusion; people killing one another in the street, his street, all trying to get away.

Two small children slept in the next room and his wife beside him, warm and still, calm.

There was a snap, a bang, like a fire cracker and a man in the house next door fell, blood gushing, like a slow mo-tion film. His body keeled over and the blood slid through the thick pullover he wore against the cold. Peter thought vaguely how it would congeal in the woollen fabric.

The blind flapped, telling him of another world, reminding him of this one.

"If only I were alone; can't risk death, my family need me. How I would run, how I would run."

"Bastard, I'll kill you." The man's face loomed at Peter, a long-barrelled rifle raised to his shoulder, a finger press-ing the trigger. Peter ducked his head, sliding under the bedclothes, and he heard the bullet buzz past.

"I'll get you." Peter's head twisted round, turning on the pillow and he saw the shot glide through the air and plunge deep into the spine of the woman struggling into the car opposite with her child.

"God, this is 1975, we're not at war, why do you kill?" He heard himself scream the words in anguish as he saw the woman's body snap backwards, her spine broken, her brain cut off, her body already shrieking for help. She slumped to the ground and her child's face showed it all. Confusion, shock.

He sweated now, anger and passion swelling the strength in every fibre. He turned, moved with the steps of a dreamer up the stairs toward the man with the gun. He seemed to stride, the world turning under his heel, his body twisting with exertion to get to the top of the steps. He grabbed the man, lifted him from the ground and in the seconds before he cast him down he saw two images. He looked to the basement where he would dash this nightmare and he saw himself lying asleep, tossing and turning, his wife, still beside him. He turned his head to one side and saw a giant. A man so tall and broad, a vast figure that stood and watched. A visitation, a dream within a dream that should not have been there. Irrelevant, but so big, so very big, and his face was broad and strong, set with a wide forehead, thick eyebrows shading piercing eyes, or at least one strange eye, for as he turned that was all he could see. Looking down, Peter saw that his hands were empty, the murderer had gone – or had never been.

He awoke with a start, turned with relief to the warm, still, peaceful body next to him. "Thank God, such things are merely dreams." His words sounded loud but real in the dark room.

Chapter 2

On a small planet named Tan-Minor sat a young varg, completely alone and waiting for nothing. He had his Porto-home boxed up beside him and vaguely fingered the button, not terribly keen to sit out in the heat, yet bored by the prospect of another day grubbing around an empty larder looking for scraps.

A varg's life really was no fun these days. There had been a time, or so the old vargs would tell, when planets were running with generosity and vagrancy was a rather special profession. A respected career. For a short comedy act or a few magic tricks, common enough skills amongst vargs, it was possible to pick up a feast and cash credits galore around these parts. Tan-Minor and even Tan-Major had always been hot varg spots, especially at this time of year when the heat made the Tans lazy and eager for entertainment.

So where were the feasts and shows, where was the money, where were the Tans? There wasn't a soul to be sniffed, not a hope of a new baked crumb. He pressed the release on his Porto-home and the force field slid round his small, tired, hungry body. Big enough to house a lone varg but nowhere the size to swing a Logomos. Still, it was home, and absolutely safe. No one could get in or out except him, and as there was no one in except him there was no danger. The young varg lay back on the force bunk and pretended to be satisfied with the idea of sleep.

He sat up with a jump, there was a line in the room, a long straight line, come in through the wall. What the Cubin devil was a line doing in his room? "Impenetrable Porto-homes" the ad. had said, before he had invested nine hundred credits in it. "Remember, when you enter your Porto-home, exactly who you are, for if once inside you should forget, you may never get out again!!!" Joke that was, how come a single line could get in and out without remembering a bloody thing? He'd return it, assuming this strange phenomenon proved amenable to negotiation. The line was thick, but with substance. It had to be some silly joke – a body squashed flat. The varg leaned from his couch to try to see the front but there was nothing. As he studied it, in the few seconds that it remained static it began to turn before him, like a picture thrown onto a screen. It expanded, spreading across the space around it, so that the line bulged and became more emphatic. The varg had never seen the like of it, for as it turned the flat thin edge was now a body. It moved from the centre of two moments in time and slipped out into his time. At last it was a man, tall, broad but skinny, hooked nose and chin, broad brow and deep-set eyes which glared down at him deliberately.

"What happens if you do that in a narrow corridor," asked the inquiring, slightly shaky varg. Gutsy fellow he was.

"I'm growing whiskers," replied the Sideways Man.

"You might at least meeow before entering, I think I shall sulk awhile, pour yourself a crom."

"Your cupboard is bare, good job you have no dog."

"I would find it croms from the table." The young varg prided himself on his repartee, but the Sideways Man seemed to tire of it.

"You should go search out Shakespeare, take a Chromohol from the Beans, they'd sell you a package deal, they'd sell you anything. But now to business, I believe you are a vagrant or, in the local vernacular, a young varg. Would that assumption be correct?"

"It might. Why?"

"Is it your hope to negotiate even before I make you an offer, are you inclined to double my intentions?"

"By doubling your intention I might double what they are."

"And what if they be death?"

"Who cares, I fear death only once, twice would be harmless."

"You are bright enough I suppose, so as you wish, one and a half times."

"Very well, I accept, provided there's crom money in it."

"A cromoholic at your tender age."

"Vagrancy needs raw guts – friend, if that is what you are."

"I'll buy you a planet and set you in a castle with credits enough to keep you in a style you are not accustomed to for a million years."

"Whose years?"

"Your own choosing."

"Old Earth?"

"'Tis done."

"What do I have to do, find the man in the moon?"

"You have to do as I will tell you. In the meantime remain here, your cupboard is full and will remain stocked until you depart without my leave. Oh, and if you do leave, well, you won't will you?"

"You haven't told me who you are yet."

"The Sideways Man."

"Gulp."

"Does that noise have some significance?"

"Yes, it means, in varg vernacular, 'no, I won't leave without your permission will I?' "

With another of his evil glares the Sideways Man reversed his arrival performance. It was the most remarkable sight for where there had been a solid, all-round man standing before the varg, suddenly with grace and practice he would turn, twisting on one foot, sideways. And as he did so his body didn't change like any normal shape but dissolved into a line. Like someone walking behind a thin post and not emerging the other side he slipped back into time, the straight line reducing to a small spot in mid air and then "pop" it was gone, without even a flurry of air.

The young varg named Vandal, collapsed into his force bed, shaky with loss of security but warmed by the sight and mouth full of crom. The Sideways man had filled every cupboard in the place.

"I wonder who invented crom,
He really must have made a bomb,
I'm glad he put some in my tum."

Vandal was prone to composing short rather silly verses. Strangely his wall recorder had more tapes of crom verse than almost anything else.

"Hello, anyone at home?" The voice issued through Vandal's internal speaker.

"No, go away, I'm busy."

"Put on your viseo, if you still want me to go then I will."

"Very . . . well, come in." Vandal's voice changed with the enlargement of his pupils. On the slightly crackling viseo was a picture of a tall, dark-haired woman, more beautiful to any eyes than most, and to Vandal, who hadn't seen, let alone had, a female for at least a year, she looked like an angel from a "gift market". She was stunning, her face slightly freckled with a fine gold and platinum headdress slanting over her cheek bones, a hair-thin ring through the muscle of her chin and a single piece of clothing which covered absolutely nothing. It was made from a material Vandal had never seen before; it changed shape and every so often slid round her body, covering parts it had uncovered, like a caressing pair of hands. At no time did it cover her superb breasts completely. Vandal had to wrench his eyes away from their high firmness, like the hills he so often climbed in his dreams, they lay still but for the occasional bob and tilt when she moved.

He put away his now second favourite indulgence and evaporated a wall. And there she stood . . . "Hello, I'm Chaos."

"I don't care how bad it is, you can sort me out, soon as you like. Sit down . . . no, don't sit down, stay standing, then I can watch you, please don't be upset if I don't look at your face all the time, there is so much else to explore."

"Oh, am I putting on weight?" She played coy and motioned her head down. With the long dark hair spilling across her shoulders she released the fine garment completely and stood naked before him. His face was directly level with thick, luxuriant, black pubic hair and he began to sweat with anticipation.

"Wh-what can I do for you?"

"Tell me about the Sideways Man."

"Uh-oh, I thought it was all too good to be true."

He slid back into the force field's arms.

"Oh, it's nothing serious, I only want to know what he said."

She stretched her arms up and her whole body moved, twisting, her hips sliding forward and then back, her legs now slightly apart. Vandal sweated more, his sense of determination in shards. Chaos kneeled down and started to untie the loops of his body tunic.

"Who . . . who are you, who's Chaos, oh, no, please . . . you . . . who?"

"Yoowhoo?"

"No, you, who are you?"

"I told you, my name's Chaos."

"Where dooooo, oh please, yes, no, where do you come . . . from?"

By now Chaos had almost stripped him.

"Oh, all sorts of places." She slid herself carefully astride him and settled gently onto his erection.

"Oh my Cubin lord help me, oh."

"Now, tell me what he said." She swayed and slipped her hips.

"Who-oooo."

"The Sideways Man." She moved her hips sideways as she spoke.

"Oh, well, oh, I'll tell you later."

"No you won't, you'll tell me now." She rose and put her strong hand on his chest, fingers pointed. "Right now, or you'll never feel the inside of another female, not ever."

"Yes, yes, I'll tell you, I'll tell you anything, only please sit down again, please!"

"Come on then." She slid back a little way.

"He, he told me to stay here, oh Lord help me . . . he . . ."

"Come now . . ."

"He told me to stay here under pain of, under pain . . ."

"Come, get on with it." She slid right back down again and began to move gently.

And he did: come that is.

"Well, you don't waste any time do you?"

"No, well, it has been rather a long time, you can hardly blame me."

"Hm, is that all he said to you?"

"Yes, that's all, I promise."

She dressed with what little there was and stepped outside again.

Vandal followed and stood slightly behind her, feeling a little churlish at her half-metre advantage over him.

"What is this life-forsaken hole?"

"Tan-Minor, it used to be full of life, now they're all gone, pissed off somewhere."

"Then why are you still here? I thought vargs could teleport."

"Oh, yes, but he dropped in while I was having a quick yawn, told me to stay put and slid off again, then you turned up. It's been a good day, one way and another."

Chaos stared across the landscape, bleak and empty with a sort of sand dune look to the hills and thick gorse bushes everywhere, there was no water, no sign of anything moving or living. Some few hundred metres distant stood a tall, gaunt tower, its walls spiralled round a central podium that was topped by a tank, presumably for water storage. It had been abandoned, left derelict. There were several structural remains dotted about, but all were crumbling, abandoned by the Tans, though Vandal knew not why.

"What date is it?" Chaos asked, turning from the dim landscape.

"Just a moment, it's . . . 2946.813, Jeso time."

Chaos noted. "How long is it since you were here last?"

"Too long it seems. About forty years ago this plain was a good-sized township, positively dancing with life it was. Those were the days."

"Hm, you sound like you're getting old, young varg, missing the past."

"Sure, wouldn't you? I had friends on Tan-Minor, now where are they? I come here, and what happens? Actually, come to think of it, I've done better since I came this time than I ever used to do."

"Oh? what in particular?"

"Don't be coy." Vandal became thoughtful and then turned to Chaos. "Something about your name, some memory, who do you sheet to sheet with?"

"Steeleye."

"Jesus Christ Superstar, that Chaos, *the* bloody Chaos, I just . . . fucked . . . Steeleye's woman."

"Correction, Chaos just fucked you."

"But you could have snapped me across one nipple and got what you wanted, why?"

"Well, why not? I quite fancied your skinny legs. Makes a change."

Vandal laughed, and laughed. "If there's a God and I'd lost my guardian angel then one returned the other today, and tomorrow he can take me away to hell and I'll tell 'em I've lived a good life and wait a million years for the next. The Sideways Man and Chaos in one fucking day."

"Tell me young Varg—"

"The name's Vandal."

"Tell me, Vandal, how long has Steeleye been around in this time?"

"Steeleye? Wow, he's . . . well, I've been hearing stories about him now for, oh, hundred and forty years, more maybe, the oldies talk about him as though he was always about. You been with him that long?"

"I was born before him."

"Eh, you're time travelling, how long have you been . . .?"

"Only ten old Earth years."

"Only ten, my old sticky armpits . . . that's really something, you ain't even a legend yet and here you are with me, hundreds of years after . . . I wasn't even . . . in fact . . . my Lord, that means . . . well, doesn't it? . . . I mean . . .

I don't exist in your own time, and yet you just . . . well, well, this'll keep them happy on Gyp for years . . ."

"Bye." And Chaos was gone.

Vandal sat down . . .

> "There was a young vagrant named Vandal
> Who never got much from his handle.
> Till 2946,
> The year of the kicks,
> The year when the dangle changed angle.
> Whoopeee."

Chapter 3

"Checkmate." Boy bounced on the couch and spat out the defeat with enormous pleasure.

"You're joking," Steeleye huffed and puffed.

"Not at all, I'm deadly serious, and you're stuck, proper stuck, not a hope in Sylva of getting out of that one, ho ho."

"Has he got you? At last." Chaos leaned over, hoping to disperse her impatience by showing interest in their Multichess, but it didn't work.

"I fear he has, little devil. We'll have to put you in for the Universal Championships."

"What Universal Championships?"

"I don't know but there must be some somewhere."

"I see, you think because I can beat the hell out of you it means I'm good enough to enter for competitions."

"Naturally, you forget, I was a child prodigy."

Boy laughed uproariously, falling onto the floor.

"Some child you were, born at the age of twenty-two."

"Who told you I was twenty-two?"

"Tousle of course, he's the only one who knows, apart from old Hamgar."

"For a ten-year-old you have some cheek."

There was silence in the huge chamber.

"God, how I wish we would get there." Chaos suddenly cursed the lack of information from their pilots, for they estimated that the journey had taken a month of old Earth time already and never a word had been heard from anyone aboard the Twin Suns.

The rooms they occupied were long, high-ceilinged, grand in style, with all manner of convenient fitments, amongst them a large bed made from the latest force field supports, which gave just the right amount according to what level of sleep you were in and how your body temperature was responding.

The heating was regulated around the individual bodies so that no one could complain of the other's self-indulgence or stoicism.

The apartment contained two bedrooms, a bathroom each, a needle shower and an atom bath, a living room, a kitchen with every device in it ever invented; and a playroom filled to bursting with games, fitness equipment, slimming devices, everything to keep the journey happy. All this inside a huge launch travelling at an unknown speed between Sylva and the mysterious Crystal Planet.

"Come my love, they will tell us when we are near, come and play chess."

"I've played a thousand games of chess and I beat you both every time. I'm sick of chess, I'm sick of all this." She swept her hand about in a dramatic gesture and as she did so a screen rose from the ground of the room and a voice sounded around them.

"We are approaching arrival, perhaps you would care to see the Crystal Planet on the Monitor. We shall land you upon the planet in two hours."

"Hooray, and about time too." Chaos leapt about the room in a dance of delight and Steeleye moved to the monitor screen.

"Come and have a look at this."

"What?"

"The Crystal Planet, it looks just like that, a crystal ball. But look it's covered in cracks, plains, as though it has been hit by a meteor and the blow has shattered it. It's beautiful, fascinating."

"Let me see, and a star too, nearby, see?"

"Yes, a moon as well, on the other side, in a different orbit."

They stood and watched their gradual approach to the planet until the star that provided this silent world with its light and heat was behind the planet, partially eclipsed.

"Wow, look at that." Boy gestured at the extraordinary result of the light through the prismatic crystal ball. Tall streams of colour rose from the surface, waving and merging continuously as the light source moved on its orbit.

"The effect that you now observe is known as the 'Ifinasis', a prismatic spectrum which results from the glass-like refraction properties of this planet. It occurs at whatever angle you are, provided that you stand directly opposite the eclipsed star and the star is not obscured by the planet's moon."

"Really getting talkative now that we're arriving," Chaos remarked. "I wonder who they are, what they look like."

"Evidently we're not to know. Or not until we land."

"Do you know what we're going to see on that planet, Steeleye?"

"No idea at all, only that it contains the source of the Circle of Freefall. I thought the place was called Freefall but it seems we are landing on the Crystal Planet."

"They are one and the same." The voice sounded again, in answer to Steeleye's question, but no one ventured into the room.

Soon they were close enough to the surface of the planet to expect immediate arrival and indeed, after a brief warning, they were teleported onto the surface with their luggage, carefully placed in a small transporter. Steeleye turned to look for the Twin Suns, but they had gone. He stood looking around them . . . He had no way of telling how far they had come or how long it had taken. He knew nothing of the planet on which they stood and his natural protective instincts were bristling, fearful of what there was in store.

The Twin Suns had gone and they were alone.

Once the "Ifinasis" had diminished to a soft corona, Steeleye could see a castle, a vast structure built in a strange mixture of styles with colossal spires and towers, jutting docking areas and one wing oddly truncated as though it had simply been sheared off. There were heads at the tops of each tower, strange heads of animals quite unknown to the new visitors.

"You are welcome to the Crystal Planet, please approach the castle, you will not be harmed, there is no danger here, we are quite alone."

The voice came from the general direction of the castle and sounded trustworthy enough so they approached, Steeleye still wary of danger, his eye burning slightly, ready for any unexpected move.

They crossed a natural jetty to a wall in which the facia had drawn apart.

As they came level with the sides of the massive walls, a small bent figure became visible against the darkness. He was no more that two metres tall and his shoulders drooped to reduce his stature still further. His hair was long silken gold and fell about his shoulders in random locks. His clothes were those of a Pierrot, long and white, falling in folds around his body.

The buttons down the front of his jacket were huge and golden; they shone and sparkled with a strange light and Steeleye wondered what could be the source of such lustre.

His face was that of an old man, except that his pupils were ovoid, and the centres were not black but quite gold, shining like the buttons on his coat.

There was no hair on his face, no eyebrows or lashes and his skin was browned a deep gold.

As he spoke he remained still, inside the door, not stepping beyond the doorway.

"I am Yellow, you are most welcome here to this castle." He turned and continued muttering, "One which I would call my own but alas the freeholder will return some day." He turned back and smiled. "Please come in."

The second they were beyond the chamber doors the entire area was filled with light. It was so large that from where they stood the far end receded into dimness. To one side there were five elevator banks with unrecognisable symbols on each.

Beyond them was a magnificent staircase which rose up through a hundred steps to slide away into darkness. The handrail was encrusted with more embossed and unknown words and signs. At the centre of the floor was a complex geometrical design, signifying something Steeleye could not unravel on sight. It was a mixture of intricate circles imposed upon a series of parallelograms and surrounded with algebraic signs.

"You are interested in the Tetrahecular?" Yellow indicated the design.

"Yes, but what is a Tetrahecular?"

"It is the translation of magic to mathematics, in that geometrical design and with the aid of the terms surrounding it you could relate miracles to sign squares, you can solve the wonders of wizardry and the sources of sorcery. I was visited once by a sorcerer, some time ago, a man in fact. He is the only living creature I've met who understood the design immediately. He explained it to me, though I have still to find use for it, even if I could, he said I would have to learn to 'see' first. Come, let me show you some of the castle."

Yellow led them from the Tetrahecular to one of the elevators and without a movement from him the doors opened, not as any doors, but in a swift roll. They seemed to curl in on themselves in one perfect turn, rolling back to nothingness and when they had entered the doors appeared simultaneously and rolled back. Everything was made to please the eye, yet there was no lack of efficiency. The inside of the elevator was the size of a large room, with softly rounded corners and lined in smooth tapestries protected by force fields. The pictures were stories of battles on land and sea and in space, of flights across many light years and against terrifying invaders.

"This is called a Cantelevator, it moves in all directions through all planes, up and down, sideways, diagonal. in a circle, or spiral, any way necessary, and it will do this for one fifth of the castle area. The other four each have their own sectors."

They reached their destination, or so it must have been, for the doors rolled back. There had been no movement, no bumps or shakes, just doors closed, and moments later, doors open.

They stepped out into a museum, another cavernous area with high ceilings and arched pillars. Immense cases filled with bizarre equipment and machines, quite unfamiliar to Steeleye, stood in serried ranks.

These machines were not metallic nor were they constructed like the computerised Exon machines familiar to Steeleye. They were spectacularly designed, one like an old theatre organ of the ancient worlds, another like a huge cabinet covered in strange heads and bodies carved from the warm, soft material. Every surface was embossed with designs and motifs. The nearest one to the curious group was like a huge bass drum, about three metres in diameter, the surface quite flat and opaque, a dull greyness on and behind it.

"What's that?" asked Boy without ceremony.

"That is one of the viewers, from here I can look into any of the Circles positioned throughout the Universe by Kimber."

"Who is Kimber?"

"The builder of this place, he built all this and more. You will hear much of him before you're through."

"So this is how you knew about Sylva?" asked Steeleye.

"Not this one, but one like it. This is an older version, there are more advanced Circles in the Circle Chamber."

Boy was rushing about the chamber from one strange device to another as if he would never see anything like it again.

"No hurry, my child. You will be here long enough to learn of all this. We have only time for a quick tour now. Come, let me show you one of the stars of the museum, over here."

They passed five tantalising specimens and Steeleye itched to ask their purpose but Yellow guided them to a very small, rather insignificant item, under a transparent cover.

"This cover, and all those you see in the museum, are quite impenetrable by force. Here, Steeleye, use your eye, see if you can break through it."

"What if I succeed? I might damage the equipment inside."

"There is no fear of that. There's a trigger device if the cover overheats, which will drop the device into a cavity below the stand. Go ahead, try."

Steeleye concentrated on the surface of the cover and beamed his eye; a strong blast made no effect whatever and so he increased power to about half maximum; still nothing.

He laid his hand on the cover, it was quite cool.

He motioned to them to stand back and concentrated the powerful eye to near maximum. It was so long since he had had to use such levels that he feared the consequences, but there were none. Somehow the power released was absorbed or diverted from the cover. There was no evidence of ricochet or damage to surrounding structures. So, maximum power. He felt the sweat on his forehead, thick beads running down his face as the beam from his eye blasted the surface of this extraordinary material. After about three minutes of bombardment, enough to wipe out a whole fleet of space launches, the small device inside the canister slowly began to lower into the stand, with smooth precision. Steeleye kept up this level of blast power in a final attack, but to no avail. The moment he cut off power the device rose smoothly up again onto the platform. He touched the cover, it was cold.

"So, you see, no damage. Though you must be congratulated, no one I have met has been able to raise the temperature of that cover by one degree. Now, let us have a look inside."

Like the other half of a comedy act, after Steeleye had been bursting his guts trying to break through the cover, Yellow simply touched a contact underneath and the cover raised itself to uncover the small machine.

Inside was a glass pyramid; a prism, and a miniature time scope.

"This is the smallest 5D prism ever developed," Yellow pronounced, as though 5D prisms had been on the market for decades.

"What is a 5D prism?" asked Steeleye and Chaos almost in unison.

"Ah yes, I was forgetting you come from Sylva. Yes, well I'll show you. Come, there's a larger one in the time chambers."

The museum had been touched upon, only two items of so many, and now they took the Cantelevator to another chamber.

A much smaller place this time. At the end of a small narrow corridor, leading off to two others, was a panelled door.

"Have you ever been in a warp chamber?"

"Like the old-fashioned time leak chambers?"

"Yes, well the other side of that door is much the same, the whole chamber is in pure warp. No mistake though, the Kimberniums discovered that a more accurate field could be set up if the time generators and time machines were themselves set in a warp."

"But what sets up the warp?"

"There's a time projector on Tristor, the moon that orbits this planet; it reflects a fine continuous time stream at this portion of the castle and keeps it, by use of various reflectors and satellites, in warp the whole time. Standing outside the castle, even if you knew where to look, you would never see this wing. Since Kimber built it and projected the time stream it has been in warp and invisible."

"And you can just walk in?" asked Boy doubtfully, as Yellow disconnected the locks.

"Yes, you can just warp in!" He smiled and roughed the boy's hair as they entered.

They all stepped into the chamber and attributed the dizziness to the warp (except Yellow who knew better). Stepping into a warp always felt like getting onto a moving stair that wasn't – a slight wobble and some dizziness.

"Within this chamber it is possible for anyone to travel to any time, anywhere from the beginning to infinity, which is the beginning. From this machine you can watch the formation of your master race, you can discover the truth about the prophet who ruled Earth for 2,000 years, you can see Jesus Christ as though he were alive today. You can transport to Itania and see the Gravels turning the planet from a grief-stricken, warring world into a paradise and then back again. You can watch Mavis Tattlebottom hang out her washing in the twentieth century of old Earth or you can see the replay of your own birth. Or, if you want to be really ambitious you can enter the Wideways."

"Tell us about the Wideways." Chaos stood beside Steeleye.

"No, I'll do much better than that. I'll take you into them right now. I spoke of the 5D prism, well, this whole planet is a 5D prism and this door, over here, is the entrance to its time shafts, the Wideways."

They walked to the centre of the first section of the time chamber which seemed to be divided into parts, each segment some fifteen metres square. Steeleye and Chaos stood together behind Yellow, all three facing the doors of time. Boy was darting around between them.

To each side of the one part of the chamber were the three elaborately decorated doors, each one large and panelled and covered in the same complex as on the stairs and elevators. There were four doors in this section, two on each side.

"The Kimberniums were great admirers of style and design as you can see, their control systems for each of these time machines are non-existent. Everything is done by thought transference, or as the Sylvans termed it 'Telepathic Insinuation'. The TI receptors are inside each door and all you have to know is where you're going. If you don't know then you will stay here until you decide."

"Are they all simple temporal fields, past and future?"

"No, this one carries you back, this one forward, and this one teleports through space and time together. This one is used for longer trips, moves faster and has some comforts inside in case you want to use it as a base when you get there."

"Where does the power come from?" Steeleye felt a little overawed by Kimbernium science.

"There is only one source, and it must have been a bit of a chance find. In 600,000 years from now there will be a most remarkable collision in this neck of the Universe. Some 1.6 parsecs away, in the Triminal system of the galaxy, two stars act as a sort of billiard cannon to an immense meteorite which manages to smack into one and bounce through the gravity fields into another. The meteorite is largely reduced to nothing, but the energy set up by the pressure movement of the two stars powers everything in this place, with plenty left over."

"How?" This made the Sylvans innocent as babes in comparison.

"Well, simple, the space time transputer has a power source from the two stars at the time of their crash and it feeds back that power in a regulated stream to the castle. It actually goes to Tristor first where the warp system begins. There's enough energy to keep us going for ever, when we get to the point where time future becomes time past then we make direct use of the space contact without time. The energy crisis from the suns will go for some while, and when it dies down the time past receptors will carry the time space connection back into operation."

Steeleye shook his head in despair.

"Yes, it is a little difficult to equal isn't it?"

"Where's Boy?" Suddenly Chaos looked around. He was gone.

They turned to see one of the time doors close firmly.

Chaos's heart almost stopped – they stood a million light years from anywhere familiar and now her crazy son had climbed into a time machine and set it in motion.

"Quick, open it." Steeleye was there before the words left Yellow's lips.

"He's gone . . ."

"Oh my Lord, what . . . what do we do?" Chaos felt as near to panic as at any time in her life.

"Wait, I can find him quite easily." Yellow touched a wall panel and a small cover quickly slid back to reveal controls and a tiny screen. Yellow watched the screen and operated the controls. "He's moving back, rather fast, now about 6,000 years old Earth time in the past. He doesn't seem inclined to organise his thoughts to stop, panicking a little, though remarkably in control for his age. Slowing down, no space locality, still on this planet, in this chamber, 6,842 years in our history. You'll have to go after him. There is no facility for getting him back. I don't know who or what is in this castle at that time, very likely Kimber himself. Come Chaos, you and I can observe the matter on the main screens."

Chaos looked back at Steeleye, doubting the wisdom of losing sight of both her son and now her man. It all seemed crazy – but there was no time. Steeleye stepped into the machine as Boy stepped out 6,842 years earlier.

Boy did not know how far back he had gone but in his mind he imagined, not without some knee-shaking, that he would simply have to leave the machine and enter another one to go forward again, rather like missing your stop on a train ride – simply get off and cross over to the other platform.

The wall on the inside of the time machine showed a date but as he knew nothing of the time scale he had left there was no use in remembering this one.

Boy opened the large door with a single touch and walked into the same world but nearly 7,000 years younger than when he stepped out. As he came out he noted that there was no change; the place was fully lit and the same doors stood opposite. It was so much the same that he half expected he might meet Steeleye, Chaos and Yellow still standing there. But there could be no Steeleye then, nor Chaos, nor Yellow.

Boy stood outside the door, quite still, looking quietly and slowly about him. There was no sign of life, no movement, no sound, no smell. He took a few steps, remembering in his agile young mind which of the doors would take him on the return train to safety. Suddenly he heard a scuffling movement from behind the partition which separated him from the next chamber. He stopped, froze, and turned his head slowly. From one side of the partition came a tall muscular figure, Steeleye.

"It's all right, Boy. You're safe now."

But before the smile could spread across Boy's face, before he could wonder how his father had arrived before him, from the other side of the same partition came a thin spiky creature. He was tall and so narrow he hardly seemed to be there. Before a moment passed he was across the gap, grabbed Boy and they were no longer in the chamber.

As he was carried away in an iron grip he felt his father's massive hand grasp at his ankle but it did no good; the hand simply disappeared.

The light of the chamber was not there, they were not there and his captor was not Steeleye.

Leaving Yellow and Chaos and climbing into the time machine to go back nearly 7,000 years, Steeleye had worked on the assumption that the time machine would know by TI reference exactly where Boy had been deposited. He set his mind to instruct arrival a few moments before Boy, so that he could be there to meet him as he came out of the machine. He arrived in fact a whole hour earlier. He checked the screen that Yellow had used in the chamber and saw that Boy was still on his way in time. Steeleye had arrived 6,842 years back, one hour before his son who started before him. He could never judge the forward time machine accurately enough to take him exactly one hour into the future again. So he would have to wait. He walked through the time chamber, debating whether he should perhaps have a quick look outside the main door and see what the castle was like 7,000 years before.

He opened the door. A sinister whirring sound came from outside. Steeleye poked his head out, twisted it one way and then the other, but he never crossed the road for in two swift glances he saw two identical robots rolling toward the door. He whipped his head back in again as they blasted, but as they did so there was an ominous crash and then another, as though the robots had been floored.

The plan was already made, he had no choice. He dashed back into the time machine and moved back a few minutes before he had arrived, came straight out, through the main door. This would have to be just right, or there could be some nasty duplications around. He hid in a small alcove and sure enough after a matter of moments the two large robots with weapons at the ready came trundling down the two corridors. Steeleye glanced at the time chamber door keeping out of sight of the robots and, as he anticipated, his own head popped out, looked one way and then the other and the robots let fly a blast at it. It popped back in again and Steeleye, in the corridor, summoned his power for an eye blast and brought them both down, one after the other, two percussive crashes of metal. No messing, he slipped back into the time chamber and watched his own figure disappear into the time machine.

Perfect. Two robots down and still a full hour before Boy arrived. He entered the Cantelevator and descended to the museum chamber of 7,000 years before. The doors opened, but not on to what he expected. Instead of an empty, vast, echoing hall he was faced by a throng of activity. There must have been somewhere in the region of two or three thousand creatures of every description in the chamber. He hesitated only a split second, reckoning that with all those already there, one more would not be noticed. There were not many of his stature but even as he stepped out no one bothered to look.

There was some kind of auction in process. The machines, or most of those that he could remember seeing, were still there and over the babble of voices was an auctioneer's hectoring. The sound of the voice came through an audio translator and Steeleye picked it up in old Earth Interlinguas. He was definitely selling the machinery in the chamber.

Steeleye looked up at the auctioneer, a straighter, taller version of Yellow. Must be his ancestor. Strange that he should be here so far back. He was very similar, just a bit younger in body, but robed the same way.

The gathering seemed important; a real feast day of activity with tables set up on trellises, food on sale and great jugs of drink. Many of the creatures looked a lot worse for wear and there were tight little gatherings sitting in corners smoking some noxious-looking rag.

The sound of the auctioneer could only just be heard above the jamboree. It was like a fair, a once-in-a-purple-moon occasion when people of all races get together and beat the hell out of the past few years. As he stood there Steeleye found himself pig in the middle to a couple of long-lost weirdest-you-ever-did-see creatures, waving long arms at one another and colliding in a passionate embrace that set them up for a real remembrance ball. He wandered amongst the crowd, all the time reminding himself of his hour limit. The machinery set in its impenetrable covers was sold off in lots of two or three every few minutes. The auctioneer, Yellow's great, great, great, great ancestor swept through his task without so much as an apology for dispensing with what was not his to sell. Each time he completed a sale large hampers of credits were passed over, all stacked in vaults behind him and quite ready, surrounded by a band of disreputable characters, to be carried off at the first word. The wise old Yellow grin that Steeleye knew was disfigured into a tired, evil grimace on this character's face.

Steeleye stopped a few yards from the auctioneer's podium and watched. The proceedings were reaching a peak of excitement when suddenly, without a word of warning, came a loud voice that boomed out of nowhere and filled the entire chamber.

"Stop."

Steeleye looked up and saw a tall thin man standing on one of the topmost pillar ledges carrying a huge blaster.

Steeleye ducked through the crowds and placed himself beside one of the Cantelevators, ready to depart. He had no wish to be splattered around the chamber 7,000 years before his coming. The rest of the crowds obeyed the authoritative command immediately and looked up in the direction of the voice.

"I will not have my museum destroyed. You shall be punished for stepping into the house of Kimbernium."

Then there was chaos. At the utterance of the word "punishment" no one waited to discover its nature. They rushed crazily in all directions, trampling each other to get out of the hall.

The tall, dominant man on the upper tower began blasting. In sprays sweeping across the floor he smattered bodies in all directions, needing no aim except downwards he slaughtered whatever came within the beam. In seconds at least half the gathering was dead. Steeleye could not interfere. He was risking enough in being there at all. If he changed the pattern of the past another atom he might throw up all manner of alterations in the future. By the time the last of the company had gone through the doors, crushed and battered on their way from death, the floor was covered with dismembered, dying and dead creatures, their life splattered on every wall and pillar. Steeleye had seen the auctioneer creep out of range the moment the killer had screamed his first command.

The carnage was horrible. The tall thin man descended to the ground, moved to one of the machines and raised the cover. He twiddled with a knob and switches, then pressed a delay switch and moved behind the machine. The catastrophic carnage vanished as though a giant with a dust pan had swept it away. Left alone were a few twisted bodies evidently still alive. All the dead were gone. The slaughterer levelled the blaster five times and killed the rest. As he did so they too vanished. A carcase disposer. Then he went to another machine and set up a force ray. Steeleye wondered for what purpose. Unless it was to prevent the departure of any creatures left in the castle.

Time was getting short now. Steeleye slipped into the Cantelevator to return to the time machine. He had just over twelve minutes before Boy was due to arrive. He transmitted TI messages to the elevator to take him back to the time chamber but somehow he sensed that wasn't where he was going. The journey seemed to be taking too long, and when the doors opened he was right. The scene before him was quite unfamiliar.

Facing him across some twenty metres of clear floor stood a giant rack; a sophisticated shelving unit. Each segment of the racking was on a slant and in each slot lay a long tubular canister, the bottom end poking out of the shelf a few centimetres, held in place by a catch. There were two hundred of these compartments and they filled the whole chamber. Steeleye tried to instruct the Cantelevator to close the doors again. He felt very uncomfortable, just waiting for something to happen, something he imagined had to be unpleasant. And he was right. The doors would not oblige and as he watched the racks the catches at the bottom row clicked and some thirty of the canisters slid slowly from their shelves to the ground, landing neatly and silently. The silence and stillness was oppressive – then the cannister on the far right began to move. It twirled, spun round on the spot, twisted rapidly and as it spun its outer layer began to peel off, the layers unravelling gradually. Then the next container began the same process, spinning round on the spot without imbalance, unwinding. And also the third and fourth and fifth and so on down the line until they were all performing the same strange sinister ritual. Then he returned his glance to the first and saw that something was emerging from inside the container. It had ceased its frantic movement and the covering was gone.

Inside was a creature, tall, about Steeleye's height and red in colour. Its body seemed translucent for Steeleye could see the racks behind outlined through the body segments. It looked faintly piscine with long twisted fins wrapped round its body, the whole covered in a slime. By now at least half had completed their revealing ritual and stood quite still awaiting their fellows. Steeleye wasted no time. He did not imagine there was to be a welcoming committee for they gave out aggressive TI responses, all directed at him. He adjusted his eye at a high level and swept the entire line with one huge blast. The first batch, those already free of their canisters remained standing, apparently unharmed. But those in the canisters shrivelled and crumpled, crashing to the ground, burnt to a cinder. Evidently they were less protected in their casing than out of it.

The first batch, about fifteen of them, unhurt by the blast, advanced and another lot came down from the other shelf behind them. Directly behind them. Those stashed near the damaged ones stayed in their shelves. They had some very rapid communication system. Steeleye sprayed the shelves, blasting at the various levels in an attempt to prevent any further attacks. He burnt up at least half of the levels, damaging the bases of the canisters beyond repair but leaving him to handle some fifteen already on their feet and fifteen more behind them preparing to attack.

The first rank advanced, fast. They wasted no time converging on the elevator doors. Steeleye had no alternative but to get out of there, and he did so, slipping to one side of the oncoming group and spraying the last four unprotected now by the new angle of fire. He killed them all. That left him with twenty-six. One of them managed to grasp Steeleye round the neck with the largest fin and the shock that swept through his body was enough to knock him off his feet. They generated an electric current so powerful that Steeleye felt his body shaking as he wriggled free of the grasp. He touched a button on his belt and shot a field round himself so that the next one who grabbed him got the shock back on itself and literally disintegrated, short-circuited. They didn't try that again but rapidly changed tactics, lashing at him with whiplash fins protruding from the base of their bodies. They appeared to have eyes set deep inside narrow sockets in the topmost part of the head section. Steeleye narrowed his own steel eye down to a pin prick and sent quick spurts of power blasted into the sockets. Three more hit the ground with a dull thud.

He ran to the farthest point of the chamber and, as he had anticipated, they all followed. They were about ten metres from him and before they got any closer he ran at them as fast as he could in so short a space and flexing every muscle in his body he crashed through. They had not expected a confrontation of this kind and like living skittles they clattered about the floor in confusion.

Steeleye made for the staircase beyond the Cantelevator and sped up ten stairs at a time. They followed.

He had no chance of finding the time chamber by foot so he rushed toward the nearest elevator and to his amazed relief the doors opened. Once inside, the machine seemed willing to obey him and moved hopefully towards the right chamber. The doors opened but in front of him all he could see was a small machine gun. It looked like the very oldest form of circular chamber machine that had to be wound by hand. It began to wind and from the barrel came short sharp laser spurts straight at Steeleye. The first made no impact on the force field but that would break down soon enough. Steeleye stepped to one side and the gun did the same. The shots continued and soon he was feeling the heat. He pressed another button on his belt and teleported behind the machine. It turned and continued to fire, still at his stomach, not missing a shot. Straight back into the elevator and off again. This was like a fun fair, fun for someone else.

The door opened once more, the twelve minutes were almost up and he rushed out into the time chamber.

"Steeleye, I presume. Welcome. You have provided me with some very considerable insight into the gaps in this castle's security system. I trust you are not hurt. Have you been here long?"

"Long enough . . ."

The two men faced each other across the time chamber, neither quite sure of the other's powers. The Sideways Man was nearly Steeleye's height, but his body was so stringy that the muscles looked as if they had been knotted by hand.

"Why did you massacre all those creatures? Is that a game you play often?"

"You've done your share of massacring too," he snapped. "It was certainly not a game, Steeleye. I am Kimber, the Sideways Man. I built this place. Those treasures in the museum belong to me."

As he spoke he paced about the chamber, very angry and disconcerted by this intrusion on his privacy.

"I discovered the Wideways and decided to explore time in them. So I left this place in the hands of that moron down there conducting the auction. His name's Yellow. I believe you have met him."

"That's Yellow, but . . ."

"Yes, I know, he's still around nearly 7,000 years from now. Well, that's his own fault."

"How?"

"You've seen the story back to front Steeleye. You started 7,000 years after it began. It began here, with Yellow, the exobiologist, 'looking after' my castle while he did his research. I return here to see how he's doing and find he's auctioning all my valuable equipment, everything, to the rabble that occupy the planets in this lousy, thieving galaxy."

"So you slaughter them. Is that the answer?"

"It's the only effective answer with rubbish like that."

"So why does Yellow stay?"

"Because he can't leave. Not now, not ever. That's why he got you in on the scene. Getting a bit bored hanging around trying to find the answers himself, so he summons a champion – the great and mighty Steeleye. Well Steeleye, just watch out, because I know all about you and if you manage to help that idiot you'll die as they did down in the museum."

They stood only feet apart, tense and unsure of each other, but a click sounded from the time door near Steeleye.

"I think your offspring is about to emerge . . ."

Boy opened the large door with a single touch and walked into the same world but nearly 7,000 years younger than when he stepped in. As he came out he noted that there was no change, the place was fully lit and the same doors stood opposite. It was so much the same that he half expected he might meet Steeleye, Chaos and Yellow still standing there. But there could be no Steeleye then, nor Chaos, nor Yellow.

Boy stood outside the door, quite still, looking quietly and slowly about him. There was no sign of life, no movement, no sound, no smell. He took a few steps, remembering in his agile young mind which of the doors would take him on the return train to safety. Suddenly he heard a scuffling movement from behind the partition which separated him from the next chamber. He stopped, froze, and turned his head slowly. From one side of the partition came a tall, muscular figure, Steeleye.

"It's all right, Boy, you're safe now."

But before the smile could spread across Boy's face, before he could wonder how his father had arrived before him, from the other side of the same partition came a thin, spiky creature. He was tall and so narrow he hardly seemed to be there. Before a moment passed he was across the gap, grabbed Boy and they were no longer in the chamber. As he was carried away in an iron grip he felt his father's massive hand grasp at his ankle but it did no good; the hand simply disappeared.

The light of the chamber was not there, they were not there and his captor was not Steeleye.

Chapter 4

Steeleye grabbed at Boy's ankle and clutched it until he felt his whole arm turn to ice and the figure that had been the Sideways Man became a thin fine line as he turned into the Wideways and was gone, neatly compressed into a spot and then nothing.

"Well, did you get him?" Yellow stood at the door as Steeleye exited back into the future.

"Where's Chaos?" Steeleye stepped before Yellow, towering above him.

"She's quite safe. What happened to the boy?"

"Kimber has him."

"Oh dear." Yellow spoke the words with real regret.

"Yes, oh dear."

"So you met the Sideways Man. I feared you might."

"Why didn't you warn me? You could have warned me."

"There was no time. I didn't realise Boy had gone there. What did you see?"

"An auction."

Yellow sighed heavily. Then turned and paced across the chamber.

"You should not have left the warp. He would never have detected you."

"Have you really been here for 7,000 years?"

"Yes."

"And you cannot leave?"

"No, not until I solve the last crossword clue."

"This is ridiculous. What in the name of Tousle will the crossword clue give you?"

"Who's Tousle?"

"Answer my question."

"The crossword is a sciento-magic device that uses the Tetrahecular and will give me the powers that the Sideways

Man has used for centuries. In the same sweep it will take them away from him."

"And you spent 7,000 years solving it?"

"Yes, 7,000 years to solve all the clues but one. That's why you're here. To solve the last one by going into the Wideways."

"If you two don't drive me crazy with all this sideways wideways stuff and nonsense . . . Where's Chaos?"

"Oh, it's not nonsense. It's very real. Chaos is in the Wideways now and you will have to go and find her before you'll get her back. She's after the Sideways Man by another route. You see I let her watch what was happening to Boy."

"I'll kill you first—"

"You cannot. In any case I am not your quarry. Kimber is."

"How am I to know?" Steeleye clutched his head. For the first time in his life he felt he was being manipulated, played with like a toy.

"Kimber has your son and Chaos is after him. If you do not go after them he will kill them both. If you wish to judge the situation you must do so after you have saved your family."

"What are the Wideways? Tell me."

"You have seen the Sideways Man. You have seen that he is solid enough when he faces you. You can walk round him and he is just like you. But when he turns sideways he slides between two moments of time and into the Wideways. The Wideways are like the light refractions of the prism on this planet. You saw them when you arrived. The planet splits light into a million streams. Well, it does the same with time. Come, the best way is for you to see for yourself."

Yellow led Steeleye into the next partition and opened a larger door which occupied one side of the chamber.

"It splits time into an infinity of dimensions, each one alongside the last and next in an everlasting circle. Get in."

"How can I trust you?"

"I need you. This is only a brief encounter with the

Wideways. You have to see the clue to the crossword yet. Now get in and you'll see."

As he stepped in he felt his movement slow down until he was completely still. Like a film replay he was unable to move but quite alive. Standing alone in the chamber, frozen into a statue.

"Now, you are in what's called the Wideways Alley. A sort of entry point from where you go through the infinite circle. It will be like looking at your own reflection through two adjacent mirrors. I'll grant you but one movement and then you'll see that movement echoed down the Wideways in all its potential alternatives. You will see what you could have done instead. Now choose your movement. It makes no difference what it is. Decide upon it and when I say, make it."

There was a moment's silence while Yellow made some adjustments. "Make your movement now."

Steeleye took one step forward and watched as he was frozen again. A spiral set in motion, starting at his body and moving out at fantastic speed. One version of his body doing something slightly different by degrees every milli-second. It spiralled away before him seemingly for hun-dreds of metres and then changed directions and curved off on another spiral, sliding back and forth, round and about for ever and ever. Across, up, down, round, each separate form seemed to be a development of the first step. The next image to him looked exactly the same – no recognisable change, and the next and next. Until what seemed a hund-red frames ahead the forward step was slightly to one side, the side toward which the foot was fractionally inclined. Then it began to move right round until he was stepping sideways and slowly overbalancing, eventually falling. Then it graduated into greater change until he was rolling and then jumping from the ground, climbing up, cavorting around doing the most elaborate somersaults. He could see all these images quite clearly until his body slowly began to turn sideways to become a fine line and then vanish altogether. There was a long gap where he appeared again in various stances only to turn sideways and vanish once more. Eventually he reappeared and was slowly gathering momentum back towards himself, performing the most elaborate physical magic, changing shape completely, and then simply sitting and thinking until it stopped, right next to him, behind his back. Everything remained, quite still.

"There, now we had better stop. The Alley is closed now. You can come out."

"I'd be interested to know why all that happened."

"According to the point at which you start the spiral, you will always get the same reaction of alternatives, but it will vary according to your entry point. There is only one set of alternatives but an infinite number of them. Each alternative that you saw is part of an entire universe within which are all the lives, planets, everything that you know of in your own Universe in essence but slightly different and more different as you progress further down the line. The choices that you understand are the nearest to you in the front of you. These exist in combination as choices in the normal Universe in which we live. But further down the line come much more complex worlds which vary from yours to a point where you could not normally have access because you lack the knowledge to get to them. In this machine it is all done for you. You can enter any one of the dimensions and travel in that Universe for as long as you please. Kimber can do it at will, without the use of this machine."

"So, as I stand here now, every millisecond that I progress the Wideways, the alternatives are there beside me?"

"Correct, the Wideways, forever sideways."

"And Chaos is in there?"

"Yes. You will find her, but first you must see the crossword."

Chapter 5

"Hic, oh they don't make crom like this any more. Where'd you get it from, Mrs Upside-down-man?"

Vandal staggered about outside his crom-fumed Porto-home, tripping through the tough grass and falling over all the bumps.

"How I wish I was really drunk. You know there used to be a time when you could get really drunk. Really really reeeeeely drunk on a single boddle of some stuff called shisky. Thas-it, whisky, scoshwhisky they called it. Made it in some place called Scoshlan or other, down in the highlands, up in the lowlans . . .

> Oh there was a young crom-swigger once
> Who had a small brain in his bonce
> They bought him some scosh
> and told him get slosh
> They had only to say it jus' once."

"Vandal."

> "Oh there was a young crom-swigger twice
> Whose body was covered in lice"

"Vandal."

> "They bought him some whisky
> and told him get frisky."

"Vandal, you stupid, half-witted varg."

"Well I must say that that wasn't nice."

"I didn't stack your cupboards full of crom to have you inebriated within a few hours."

"Yeshir, no shir, Mrs Upside-down shir."

"Stand up or I'll take what's left away."

"I'm here, I'm here. Don't make threats like that. I'm as sober as a Tansinian Masker, what do you want?"

The crom effect wore off with the threat of crom deprivation.

"Good, now I want you to look after this boy."

"Boy? What's a boy?"

"This is a boy and his name is Boy."

"Where's Tarzan—?" Vandal put out a hand.

"Don't you touch me." Boy backed off sweeping the hand away with a gesture.

"Touch you, touch you – me? I wouldn't touch a boy. Not in a million years of castle dwelling. Sire, who is he?"

"Never mind. Just look after him. You let him get away and I'll stuff you into one of those empty crom cans like a genie into a magic bottle. Understand?"

"Understood, all present and correct, Mrs er Mr you can rely on old Vandal."

"I hope so. Just don't let anyone lay hands on him right?"

"Right, right, right. Come on, Boy, come and have some crom."

"What's crom?" asked Boy snootily.

"Don't be snooty about crom. It's the best thing since scosh."

"You mean Scotch, I presume." Boy sat on the small rock beside the Porto-home.

"You may presume what you please. I says what I mean, and I mean scosh. You call it what you want." Vandal squatted, trying to sound superior.

"It's correct name is Scotch whisky."

"Correct? Who wants to call things by their correct names? Correct names are boring. Scotch whisky is boring. Scosh is better. Boy is boring, Yob is better."

"You can't call me Yob."

"Why not? Do you know what it means? Yob?" Vandal stood up again, taunting.

"It means, er . . . well, something rude or you wouldn't have said it."

"Well, you look a bit like a teddy bear so it'll make a perfect name, Yobo, come on, Yobo. Don't mess with me, baby, 'cos you'll be sorry."

"I'll punch your stupid squashed nose if you call me that again."

"Call you what?"

"Yobo."

"You said it, not me, punch your own nose, Yobo." Vandal danced about.

"Right." Boy swung a well-aimed punch and caught Vandal square on the nose.

"Ouch, you little scamp. I'll . . ." The young varg made a lunge at Boy but Kimber caught him by the collar.

"No you won't Vandal. You'll treat the child well. He's got courage and he's Steeleye's son . . ."

"Stee . . . proper bloody family gathering."

"What?"

"Nothing." Vandal realised he had said too much.

"What did you say? Has Steeleye been here?" Kimber shook him.

"No, certainly not."

"Then who, who has been here? Tell me or I'll snap you with my fingers, Varg." He pulled him up to his own height.

"Chaos."

"When?"

"Immediately after you."

"So she's in the Wideways."

"The what?"

"Where's your home planet?"

"What home planet?"

"Don't fool with me, Vandal. The Gypsy Planet, where all you scruffy lot get together and plan your next binge."

"Hm, I'll tell you anything, but I won't tell you that. It wouldn't be worth my life."

"Your life won't be worth much anyway if you don't do what I tell you. Take him there. Take him to the Gypsy Planet, tonight."

"What? This boy? They'd eat him for supper."

"Well, don't let them. You tell them he's mine. That'll stop any pestering."

"I can look after myself, thank you," Boy piped up bravely.

"Not on the Gypsy Planet you can't," Vandal parried, but Kimber's strong hand tightened around his throat. "All right, only I don't guarantee he'll come back in one piece."

"If he doesn't, then you won't either. I shall see to it personally." And with those friendly words the Sideways Man was gone into the line of departure.

Vandal blew a raspberry.

"Stupid skinny old crow." He stomped into the Portohome for another can of crom and then leaned out again.

"Don't get any clever ideas about escaping, Yobo, because there's nowhere you can go from here, up, down or sideways, and if you hit me again I'll piss off and leave you. So, drink crom and be friendly or sit on your own and sulk."

"I'd prefer the latter, thank you."

"I'd prefer the latter, thank you," Vandal mimicked. "Suit yourself.

They sat in silence for a moment.

> "There was a young fella named Boy
> Who sat around feeling no joy.
> This was no surprise,
> For I tell you no lies,
> He'd forgotten to bring his best toy."

Vandal fell about laughing, and eventually Boy smiled slightly and began to laugh too.

"Listen, Yob, er Boy, if you're coming to Gyp with me you've got to look like a varg."

"What's a varg?"

"A vagrant."

"You mean a tramp."

"No, a vagrant. A tramp has no skills, a drop-out. A vagrant is deliberately freeing himself from the society he lives in. There are millions of us, have been for centuries and we've got headquarters. Very well organised we are, like a union where we meet now and again and it's called Gypsy Planet. I call it Gyp. And no one is allowed there who isn't a certified vagrant. So we've got to do something about those neat little clothes you've got on. We've got to rough you up a bit. Come in here, I've got an old jacket you can put over the top."

"What will they do with me when we get there?"

"Nothing, if they think you're a varg, nothing at all. Vargs are free to come and go as they please, so don't give the game away because they can get a bit nasty if they think there's a spy in the camp. Here, put this on. Just a minute, let's put a tear in that top you got on." Vandal ripped the fabric. "That's better. Now a bit of dirt on the face, like so, and a bit under the nails like so. Your name's all right, sounds suitably vargish. O.K. what about a history? We'll have to give you a background in case someone starts asking you questions."

"If they ask me questions I'll just tell them to mind their own business."

"Yes, that's all right at first but you might have to give some information at some stage, and if you ain't got none it'd be a bit embarrassing now wouldn't it? Can you fight?"

"Try me." Vandal swung a punch and Boy neatly swept the blow away and delivered a punch to the ribs followed by a kick which seemed to come round the back of Vandal's body from nowhere.

"Here, where'd you learn to do that?"

"It's called Tai Chi Chuan, an ancient Earth martial art. Steeleye taught me. I'm a master of it."

"So we call you Master Boy, do we?"

"If you like, another Tai Chi fighter would."

"Think yer pretty smart eh? I just hope you don't get too big for your smart boots on Gyp, that's all."

"I'll be careful."

"Yes, you be careful. Now give me those boots and we'll see if we can mess them up a bit."

No one ruled the Gypsy Planet. There was no central command, or administration buildings. No arrival ports, no welcome committee or governmental seat. In fact there wasn't a seat of any kind that belonged to the planet. There was nothing other than a small dumping ground near the northern pole belonging to this desolate squatter's world. The vargs brought their goods with them, each one carrying his chosen habitation, whether it be a brown paper parcel tied by string or an elaborate Porto-home. There was no status, no authority except that of the weapon or the tongue, no love gained or lost, no trust given or taken, only individuals who gathered on the planet when they chose. There were always some few hundred dotted around at any given moment so that a travel-weary vagrant could be sure of a warm fire and a chat, provided he could supply at least a story or two. No one else was either welcome or tolerated. The thin, barren wasteland, occupied this night by several hundred varying vargs, was scattered, like a battle camp, with fires and small groups formed at random. The creatures, all shapes, colours and sizes, were strikingly varied, but all seemed able to communicate, or if not, sleep or listen to the sounds that issued from their fellow vargs. There was no restriction on race in the vagrants' community. Except that you had to be registered as a varg, there was no restriction whatsoever.

To begin with the night had no particular significance in the varg's diary, nor were there many vargs about. There was no particular event scheduled and no one had any story likely to raise a varg's eyebrows, if he had any.

"Now remember what we've been through, who you are, where you came from. Don't get angry if someone has a go at you. It happens all the time and for the sake of the Cubin devil don't get up on that high horse of yours and start telling them where to get orf, right?"

"I suppose so."

"Yes, well you bloody well go on supposin' so, because if you don't your supposin' days will be numbered, right?'

"Right."

"Right. Now, I can see one or two buddies of mine. I think we'd be better off round their fire. Come on."

The Gypsy Planet was bleak, chosen deliberately for its unwelcoming atmosphere. It had once housed some community, many thousands of years before, but no record remained of the life forms who had left such a mire of filth and dirt behind them; dark blue clouds of dust that fell every few hours, and nights that lasted for two-thirds of the true round.

Altogether a strange planet, unpretentious, unwelcoming, unprepossessing, simply un- most good things.

"What a pong."

"What do you mean what a pong? What's a pong?"

"You mean you, of all people, don't know what a pong is?" Boy almost burst out laughing, but as no one else seemed to be even near a snigger he stifled it.

"No, I don't know what a pong is. Now supernut, tell me what a pong is."

"A bad smell." Boy pretended to duck.

"If I didn't think I'd get a smack in the chops I'd give you a brisk good hiding. Of course there's a pong. That's because we don't have needle showers and atom baths on Gyp and we manage to avoid finding too many natural springs in the mountains, so we tend to get a bit smelly now and again, and you will too little Lord Steeleye, because you ain't going to see the inside of a bath for a few weeks I shouldn't wonder. Dont worry, your nose'll soon get accustomed to the, er, 'pong'."

"Now come on, let's go and meet my buddies. Just remember yourself, keep your gob tight shut unless they prise it open, right?"

"Right."

"Vandal." The greeting as the two newcomers sat, squat, by the fire was perfunctory.

"Storm. Brought a friend, lost outside varg country, no Porto-home."

"Greetings . . .?" There was only the merest hint of query in the voice, which issued from a head-cloaked figure seated, back bent beside Vandal.

"Boy." Boy gathered the down-tone speaking and reciprocated,

"Been mixing recently?" The question, according to the slight drop in volume was directed at Vandal, so Boy sealed up again, relieved to be out of the conversation.

"Huh, yes, free crom and a screw, all in a day's work. How about you?"

"You jest with me, Vandal. I am in no mood for jest."

"No, I do not, Storm. But tell me, what problems?"

"Plier's been here, singing songs of times to come."

"Varg times?"

"Sure enough, Vandal, varg times, all times."

"Like what times?" Boy listened intently.

"Two space racers and a third. A visitation, your name was mentioned. We know about Boy."

Vandal spluttered, swallowed, tried to speak again but decided silence was better. He put out a hand and gripped Boy's wrist so tight he had to swallow a cry.

"Sit tight, the old vargs are deciding."

The visitation from Plier was significant. Plier was the oldest varg and had definite premonitory gifts. He came very rarely but when he did it was invariably to warn of forthcoming events.

"Is Plier amongst them?" Vandal finally asked.

"Yes, he details, something about a fight. We are to help. No names yet, except one."

"Mine?"

"Yours is ours. No, this is an outsider, but . . . good enough for us, good enough for us . . ."

"Who?"

"Steeleye."

Boy drew breath sharply and for the first time Storm turned to look at him. The bent, hooded figure turned and the hood opened to reveal a face rarely seen. It was battered and misshapen, with one eye clean gone and the other enlarged as if to make up the loss.

Storm had a reputation amongst vargs for trust and strength, both rare varg qualities. His physical tenacity was enormous, stringy and bare to the bone his body could grip another and squeeze all life out of it. But he kept his word and could always be relied upon if he gave his word – an exceptional varg.

"The old ones will assess the potential for vargs and call

a Big Talk. You're O.K. Boy will live too, but we need to know what's about."

"Have we sent out spies?"

"Yes, they tell of Kimber and Yellow."

"The old feud. I saw the Sideways Man but he feared only Steeleye. No mention of Yellow."

"Go tell the old ones. They need to hear."

Much to Boy's horror Vandal got up and left the gathering.

The fire glinted and darted across the dour gathering. No one spoke. After what seemed hours of waiting and black silence an ancient varg stood, crouched in the night's half light. The jumping fire flickered across his crippled body, the heat haze changing his shape with each gust of wind.

"Vagrants, we are decided that Plier's words be listened to. We expect a visitor, his name is Steeleye. We shall respect the life of his son Boy who is amongst us and Vandal shall be blameless."

The old fellow sat again and slowly talk began round the firesides. Vandal returned to his place.

"How do they know, how does Plier know?" Boy was jumpy with questions.

"Don't ask me. He knows, what he says, they always listen to him. I thought it would be peaceful here. Wrong again, and the old feud too."

"What old feud?"

"Yellow and the Sideways Man. They've been at it for thousands of years, ever since Yellow tried to ransack the Crystal Planet. Now Yellow has pulled your dad in on the act and apparently he's going to come here, though he doesn't know it yet."

"What for?"

"You, of course. What else?"

"What, but Storm said it was good for the vargs."

"Yes, he did. So, I guess it will be. We'll see won't we?"

Yellow led the way, after they had left the Cantelevator,

down a series of very dark, ancient corridors, a good deal too low to accommodate Steeleye's bulk with ease.

"Keep your head down. I'd hate to see that eye smack a stone beam."

"Wouldn't hurt the eye. It's protected. How much further?"

"Nearly there. Just a few more turns. Kimber hid the crossword box as far away from the centre as he could. It took me a long time to dig it out. Last turn."

They rounded another bend and took one of five different alleyways. This one ending with a small panelled door with no symbols or indication of its contents. Yellow touched one of the stone wall blocks to one side of the door and then another spot on the other side. The door slid open a fraction. Yellow moved his hand across one of the door panels and touched another point at the centre of the door. It opened, sliding into the wall, another few inches, until there was space enough for a thin body.

"If I squeezed in now the door would shut on my body and drive me into the panel in the wall, crushed to pulp. Devious fellow Kimber. It took me a fair while and a couple of pocket computers to solve this little bit of trickery."

Yellow then touched the outside edge of the door in one spot and it moved another few inches. Before it stopped, and evidently at a precise moment Yellow pushed the centre of the door hard and much to Steeleye's surprise the door began to shut again and open the other way, sliding decisively into the wall on the other side.

"See what I mean? Silly games to make life that little bit more difficult. Come in, it won't shut now till I tell it to. And that was no joke either, changing the closure voice patterns."

"Wouldn't be much fun getting in there quickly would it?"

"Oh, there is a quick way but I haven't fathomed that out yet, haven't needed it thus far. Now over here."

The chamber was small, only just a few inches above Steeleye's head and some twelve metres square. There was nothing in there but a single podium with a box standing upon it, heavily embossed with intricately mounted jewels. Its top was set out like a small crossword puzzle.

"This is it. The great Kimbernium crossword. Locked in this box is the power of the Wideways. Solve all the questions and you can travel in time, forward, backwards, upside down, sideways, from infinity to infinity without aid or device. At this moment there is only one living creature with that gift and that is the Sideways Man . . . Kimber himself. He solved the 5D prism problems, set up the Wideways travel and he alone knows how it is done."

"And if you solve the crossword, does that give you the power too?"

"No, it gives me the power alone. Only one person can travel in the Wideways at any given time without aid. Don't ask me why, it's just so. Once I have the answer to the last question, Kimber will be deprived both of his castle and his gift."

"And you will be free to leave this place?"

"Yes, at last."

"I see, and what is to stop me keeping the power for myself? If I have to solve the question, why can't I have the power?"

"Because you don't know the answers to the rest of the crossword. I do."

"I see, but I shall know the most important." Steeleye spoke this quietly, and Yellow did not hear.

"Now, let me show you the question, then we can get you on your way." They stood before the box.

"Final question." Yellow spoke the toneless query to the air.

And from the air came the answering question.

"Pon the Storms of Wander-land,
See, the gatherings know.
There is where the powers lie,
Where time its seed does sow."

"Would you like me to give you a memorecord of that? Oh, no, forgive me, you're well equipped for things like that, aren't you? Good, come then, now you can get into the real Wideways."

"And where do you suppose I'm going to start?"

"Well, I suspect that is your own problem, Steeleye. You after all are the genius. Go now, solve the problem and return, then you can have your woman back and with luck your son."

Chapter 6

"Ever played paperchase?"

The question hung in the TI patterns that spun round Steeleye's head as he stepped into the Wideways proper.

Ever played paperchase? What could it mean? The intonation was familiar. It came from . . . of course, from Chaos – she had left a message, a paperchase message.

Immediately after the first thought came another.

"Watch a vagrant on Tan-Minor, but stay in the Alley. It has a purpose, you might even enjoy it."

The taunting, slight note of coyness sent shivers down Steeleye's back. She was up to her tricks.

Steeleye sent out the TI orders and felt his body twist along the Wideways alternates, changing as he went, until he arrived out of the spectrum of changes and into a new universe. The Kimbernium time machine carried Steeleye through the Wideways without his needing any knowledge of his destination other than its name.

Tan-Minor existed in a dimension far from his own, and several hundred years into the future so that Steeleye was by then well known to the many worlds, places he had not yet even seen. Such were the confusions of time travel.

He stayed in the Wideways Alley and watched as he projected forward along the temporal channels of this dimension. Soon, a small figure flashed by teleport onto the surface of the sandy, rough-grassed world, sat down and laid a Porto-home beside him. He seemed depressed, lonely, and soon disappeared into the force home. First came the Sideways Man who spoke riddles to Vandal and was gone. Then Chaos arrived, materialising out of nowhere to signal her arrival to the fellow in the small structure.

"What's she up to?"

He watched Chaos entice the small creature inside the

home, and slowly, very excitingly seduce him. Steeleye's feelings were mixed, about fifty per cent jealousy and fifty per cent amazement. There she was, gaily making love to some nasty little beast on a planet far enough away from Steeleye to be safe, except that she had told him about it and must have known he was watching . . .

"You might even enjoy it" he said. "Hm, have to have a word with her about this lot . . . " He continued to watch until Chaos had dressed and departed . . .

As she went another TI message floated across the air to Steeleye's receptors.

"Soon enough, Kimber arrives again! But leaves Boy, so do not touch. Vandal's unaccustomed erection carries a tracer. Follow and we shall meet where he goes."

Steeleye wondered at his woman's guile. He waited in the Alley until the Sideways Man arrived in Tan-Minor with his son, dumped Boy with Vandal and departed. Sure enough Steeleye was picking up signals from the crom-happy varg.

Vandal took Boy's hand in his, placing a clasp about his waist, and set up the teleport co-ordinates that would carry him to Gyp. The tracer gave Steeleye the numbers and he fed them into his own teleport device.

He experienced the usual slick jerk that snapped his body into a disrupted state and started the strange journey across the no time of space.

He rematerialised in the same dimension, in orbit about a planet that suited the strange scraggy little creature who had carried Boy away. It was so isolated that the star nearest to it seemed to be straining to cast light and heat on this lost world, far from its influence. From what Steeleye could see there was little if anything to commend it. Nevertheless, this was where the riddle told of answers to the crossword puzzle and Boy was there.

But where was Chaos? As Steeleye muttered the words to himself, a line appeared before him in deep space. It was white, clear and full, long and quite straight. Slowly it emerged into a shape, a shape so different from the straight line that Steeleye's pupils enlarged with excitement. This was a woman, a real woman, turning out of the Wideways before him. Chaos stood there, slowly facing him. She walked forward, her hips swaying and Steeleye was reminded with a jolt how long it was since he last held her. They kissed.

"We have work to do." Chaos uttered through quick breath.

"Huh, I've read that line somewhere."

"Our son is down there, in the hands of those creatures. They hardly look the friendliest bunch, do they?"

"I don't know. The riddle spoke of a Wander-land."

"What riddle?"

"The crossword that Yellow so badly wants solved."

"Tell it to me"

" 'Pon the Storms of Wander-land,
See, the gatherings know.
There is where the powers lie,
Where time its seed does sow."

"Explain."

"I haven't sorted it all out yet, but if this is Wander-land, then the riddle says they know what's going on already, which supposes they are expecting us. Time has sown a seed, that means they also know about Yellow and Kimber perhaps, because it's been going on for a while. I don't understand the reference to Storms, this is not what I'd call a volatile climate!"

"If they're expecting you it doesn't necessarily mean they're going to be friendly."

"True. But the third line says 'there is where the powers lie'. That can only mean that I'm going to get the answer to the puzzle through them, right?"

"Possibly, but who's going to get the power from this crossword. Yellow, Kimber or you?"

"Hm, who knows – Yellow holds most of the trump cards."

"Except the vargs."

"Except the vargs, yes, perhaps they are the link. Come then, we'd better see what they have to offer. Cover yourself, full force, I don't want that beautiful body marked."

Boy had watched many times, in the days on Zrost, the "Old Times" as Tousle would call them. The times when men would fight men, hand to hand across vast plains of mist and desolation. The camp where he sat, cross-legged, smelled of lost people, quiet with the sound of empty air, hanging loosely from bent head to bent head. No one spoke. No real sound uttered in the semi-darkness; everyone tensed and over-aware, like parachutists waiting for the drop. Boy had seen them too. He had been there, to old Earth, in the times of the great Wars, long before Tousle, or any robot. The same mixture of apprehension and energy lifted from each present that night, an evening that had begun without event was suddenly the outer ripples of a vortex. Boy thought of how so often, time seemed to hold events at arm's length while it reorganised matters to its own satisfaction and then replaced them like an intricate jigsaw back onto the air, neatly synchronised. But how hard it was to see them shape when you were amongst them. Like colour shafts on the Crystal Planet, watching from above must have been so logical and coherent but standing in the long grass of light was total confusion. That is how he had felt on his journey with the Sideways Man through the Wideways.

The fires burned and the flickering flames cracked at the dry wood and shrub gathered by the vargs. The night air was full of heavy dew and steam curled off the bodies of the vargs and the fires dropped, smoking with the dampness. Then Vandal looked up and so also did other heads. To one side of the camp a bright blur of light came through the mist, forming slowly into the shape of two figures inside one outline of force. The turning of the force atoms around their bodies caused the air to glow slightly, giving them an unreal majesty which enhanced the image of Steeleye and Chaos descending god-like to the ground.

They stood on the outskirts of the groups and watched in

silence for a short while. Then Boy saw a tall figure rise from his own fire, a creature far taller once standing than he had looked sitting on the ground, doubled up, his arms across his knees. He was completely covered, hooded and caped to the ground.

"Welcome, Steeleye. I am Storm. Please enter our encampment. We have been expecting you."

"The clue to the riddle. You are 'the Storms of Wanderland'."

"So the box has been found, and they are fighting over its power. Follow me, you must meet our elder. He is called Plier, my father Plier."

Steeleye sat, cross-legged opposite Plier and his son Storm, and other elders sat either side. The fire snatched at the wood between them. Chaos shivered involuntarily at the strange darkness of the atmosphere. She pressed a button on her belt and increased a fine wave of heat around her body.

"We are glad to have you with us, Steeleye and Chaos. We have mapped your progress with interest. We are aware of your quest and the questions of the crossword box on the Crystal Planet. As vagrants it is our profession to inquire."

He paused, staring into the fire, as though searching for answers.

"The answer to the question that Yellow has asked you to solve does not exist. There is no question and no answer. There is only you and us. A number here are destined to wrest the power from Yellow and the Sideways Man, to travel in the Wideways, and we are destined to do it only with your leadership. It is written and told in our history, our history of the future."

"Tell me of your readings?" Steeleye asked.

"It is told in varg mythology that a Man of Steel will take us to task and through his power and energy will give us even greater power and energy and will take us, many of us, on greater adventures through the stars than ever in our history. It speaks also of the Wideways, 'The Powers of the Prisms of Time, the Sideways Dimensions' and many things that are released to the holder of such powers. The new holder will be you, Steeleye, for Kimber has overstayed his sovereignty in the Wideways. But there is much to do to fulfil that prediction. We are dealing with the Wideways and in the Wideways anything can be changed – even the predictions of Varg."

The Wideways are like the corridors between mirrors. Set two large mirrors opposite one another, precisely opposite, so that the reflective qualities are perfect. Now stand between them and you will see an infinity of corridors like the one in which you are standing. But have you ever tried to step out of your own corridor into the next, through the mirror? Or have you ever thought that perhaps you are not in that corridor but in one of the others already, or all of the others? Which one is the real you? They all pinch themselves when you do, they all laugh in derision when you mock their reality. Who is to say they are less real than you? Who is to say that two such mirrors are not in fact a view of the Wideways? Who is to say indeed, for they are.

Walk out of the reflection view, beyond the point of the mirrors and the others will do the same. Does that mean they no longer exist? Certainly it doesn't. They too are walking away from their mirrors into their own world which is very different from yours. The only identical factor is the mirrors. They all have two mirrors placed apart in a corridor. When you step between them, they do exactly the same because the alternatives are precise, there is no change at that point in your existence; no alternative but the same one. In that moment of infinity they have the same mirrors and do the same act. At every other moment they are different.

The effect in the science of the Wideways is called an "Identic-alternative". There are other such moments but most are outside the general precinct of our everyday experiences.

In the castle on the Crystal Planet there were two such mirrors. They measured three metres in height and five in width and stood in one of the wide corridors that joined one chamber to another. Yellow was walking down that corridor a few moments after he had despatched Steeleye on his way into the Wideways when he stopped and turned, involuntarily, to look into the mirrors. It had always been an ambition of his to be able to walk through the mirrors at any moment, without the help of the Wideways time machine. He stood and mused on the future possibility, that he might one day soon be able to do just that. And as he looked a tall fearsome creature appeared behind him. He turned, but no one was in the corridor with him and when he looked more carefully the figure, heavily cloaked, was only in one of the reflections behind him, in the Wideways in fact, some thirty or forty reflectors away, alone and unrepeated.

Yellow left the mirrors for a moment, unsure and frightened – he went to the museum chamber. There were many devices in the castle which Yellow and Kimber alone understood. Yellow moved to a large console on one side of the museum and raised the protective cover. He played with a number of controls and there were changes within hidden parts of the castle, unheard and unseen, but decisive, and ensuring greater protection to its occupant. He set up all the monitor screens and primed and tested all the many blasters set into the walls.

Yellow then made his way back to the mirrored corridor and again approached it, this time more cautiously. Until he was between the mirrors he could see nothing, but, once there, he froze in his tracks. Standing one way and then the other he saw no less than four figures now in the Wideways, two either side. The original traveller was as he had been before, but now, in front of him stood three more, on each side of the corridors, closer than the first one. And as he watched came two further arrivals. Now there were six and each one had taken up the same stance, legs apart, gaunt and shabby in appearance, one stage nearer.

"Who are you?" Yellow spoke calmly, knowing that they might not hear him, but feeling at a loss to fathom their intention. There was no answer, no movement. They stood there, it seemed scarcely alive. Their faces, those he could see under the deep hoods, were scarred and thin, dirty from what must have been months without care. They were all tall, taller than him, straight-backed and young. Their bodies were hidden under the cloaks which revealed neither limbs nor weapons. Who knows what was hidden beneath those heavy folds? "Do you wish to speak with me? Are you lost? Can I offer you refreshment or aid?" Still no response. Then two more. Each one arrived, walking slowly into his corridor, casually taking up the still position and standing there, now eight and the nearest one but twenty-six corridors removed from Yellow.

For the first time in so many hundreds of years Yellow felt real doubt and fear, mixed like a potent poison in his mind. The appearance of them would not have been so bad, but it was their mute silence that distressed him. Why did they not respond?

Many things could happen in a world where millions of other worlds passed by, where the Wideways opened passages to infinity, but never before had he encountered such a sinister bunch. He left the mirrors and went to the time chamber.

He lifted the hatch which covered the Wideways time machine controls and turned on the screen. The many channel switches which gave him access to anyone travelling in the Wideways were flashing. He knew that there was Steeleye and Chaos in the dimensions using this machine but he had not imagined there could be anyone else.

"But of course, Steeleye has let them in. Steeleye has brought these creatures in, or they have entered themselves through his access."

He pressed a button and twelve lights flashed on. There were ten living beings in the Wideways channels other than Steeleye and Chaos. So the mirrored passengers were now ten. Then two more, twelve, and increasing all the time.

"What's he doing? Why is he bringing them here and why by the back door?"

He pressed open another channel. This one allowing him

speech access to Steeleye, Chaos and the others in the mirrors downstairs.

"Steeleye, Chaos, I would welcome a report on your progress. I have a number of visitors in the mirrored corridors and would be happier if you could introduce them to me." Fourteen now. "Steeleye, can you hear me?"

"Yes, Yellow, I can hear."

"Where are you? Give me a reading of your position."

Steeleye knew that if he told Yellow where he was it would be easy for him to freeze him into the Alley of the Wideways.

"I cannot do that, Yellow, for I wish to remain mobile. I don't want you putting me on ice. You'll just have to guess."

"You know I cannot do that, and I hoped that you might trust me a little more than you appear to. But never mind, tell me, why do I have suddenly to contend with so many visitors, not very friendly ones either."

"They are friends of mine, Yellow. You need not fear their arrival. They will not harm you, provided you do not fool with anything in the castle that might damage our mutual future."

"You speak in riddles, Steeleye. What should I fiddle with? I await your return with *our* answer. Or have you found it and will not tell me? Are you ambitious, Steeleye, on your own account? I would not advise it, there is nothing you can do with your answer without me or . . . "

"Or what Yellow?"

"You aren't by any chance in Kimbernium are you?"

"No, Yellow, a long way from Kimbernium. A long, long way. But I have been there, briefly, just to pay my respects to the people who threw out your adversary. They spoke much about you and the Sideways Man, much about your long feud."

"Come back here, Steeleye. Come back and help me to solve the clue. I promise you will not regret it. You will be rich and powerful and we will dispense with Kimber together.

"Oh, I shall be a little while yet, Yellow. Sit back, you've waited this long. You can wait a little longer. Chaos and I are enjoying ourselves. We're having a holiday. I've found the answer by the way, so don't do anything silly or you might never get it."

"Can't you tell me now. Tell the answer, Steeleye, please . . . " Yellow's voice trembled with anticipation.

"Can't do that, Yellow. Keep going. I'll try and get back as quick as I can. Might even make it in a few moments of your time, so you won't notice. See you soon . . . "

"Steeleye, please, the answer . . . "

"Bye . . . " The voice trailed away. Yellow tried to bring him back onto the console but without success.

There were eighteen of Steeleye's mates now in the mirrors.

Yellow sat silently for some while and then with a look of determination he rose from his seat and strode out of the warp chamber. Moments later he was wheeling a large contraption on a trolley towards the mirrors. Once between them he stopped, looked at the twenty vargs in the corridors and turned a switch. A slight haze fell over the two mirrors. He might not be able to get at them, but he could effectively stop them from getting at him.

"You can tell your Steeleye friend that he might be clever, and he might be strong, but he should never declare his intentions, for Yellow's no fool either." With that he stomped out of the mirrors.

Chapter 7

"We need a launch!" Steeleye stood beside Chaos, Boy and Vandal, on Gyp.

"You are looking at the arch launch half-incher, I'll have you know. There is no one of greater skill in the Universe. I can pick, blast or tinker my way into anything that takes off, or anything that doesn't for that matter."

"What is a half-incher?"

"You're not listening are you? What I said was, if you want a travelaunch of any description, I'm your varg."

"O.K., so where do we start?" Chaos smiled down at Vandal.

"There's a nice flourishing planet near here called Bantam. Storm says there's pickings there. Good a place as any to start looking."

"Storm was right. Just look at this place. It's bursting with goodies." Vandal stalked from one side of a building, preparing to deprive a local inhabitant of his purse. Steeleye grabbed his tunic and hauled him back.

"We're here for a launch, Vandal, not a few credits. The nearest space port is in that direction."

"O.K., O.K., just thought we might need some cash."

"Come on." They left the small centre of a town on Bantam. One or two inhabitants looked at them doubtfully, for they were a motley bunch, but no one seemed concerned enough to hinder their progress. Bantam was very small, compact and rich in important minerals. It also had the Galactic Patent on a neat little launch security system, though Vandal knew nothing of this. The space port was disproportionately large for so small a population, with modern craft lined up, each one with its own attendance unit of repair and overhaul robots.

"Are you sure about getting hold of one of these? They look pretty well guarded to me." Steeleye looked over the bright clean systems that surrounded the launches and imagined, rightly, that bright clean systems meant bright clean security.

"Ah, but your eyes are inexperienced in such matters. I can assure you there are more complex launch sites than this in the Universe."

Vandal crept forward to crouch just outside the limits of the dock units. The others followed. Steeleye had his doubts but could think of no other method of getting a launch, and they had to have one if they were to get to Carosh. Yellow's planet was much too far to teleport four in one.

"Right, now prick up yer lugs. This is what we do." They went into a huddle and Vandal fed out the orders.

He stood straight, wrapped his cloak around him and pulled the hood up so that no part of his head or body was visible. He took a small laser gun from Steeleye's belt and walked straight into the launch port area.

There was no movement from any of the robots and there seemed to be no sign of a living attendant, which meant the security systems were automated.

Without warning he turned towards one of the launches, one that he had picked out as the most powerful. It was a Kaiserverner Medium Flight, one of the fastest space launches. Its normal space energy capacity would be in the region of 180 megatons and it would have teleport capacity, space/time anti-matter generators, and all mod cons. It would also be bloody difficult to get into without a key! He knew that there would first be a force field to prevent anyone other than the owner of the craft from entering the dock. That was no problem.

"Robot. Message for transference." He spoke with authority, standing just outside the field, aware only of the slight magnetic tingle that it set up in the air. The robot advanced and cleared the field to take the message disc which Vandal held before him.

At the very instant the field was cleared a fine, sharp

beam severed the robot's motor control channels so that it could not move a muscle. It stood stock still as ineffectual as a statue. Vandal entered the dock and closed the force field to his own co-ordinates. Now no one could get in or out except him.

The second robot was only a technician and presumed that if Vandal was there he had a right to be.

Vandal made his way to the force elevator and touched the contact. He was whisked up to the control doors which were shut.

He stepped onto the platform. "Now let us see what we shall see, shall we? Yes, let's . . . " His senseless mumblings reassured him. He took a small pair of earphones with a long wire attached to them and placed the end of the wire onto the door, near the lock. He listened to the quiet ticking and tumbling of the security systems, from which he hoped to identify the locking mechanism's origination. "Funny, never heard one like that before." He turned the volume on the audio set up to maximum and recorded the sound of the lock. He touched a button on the earphone, took the sucker off the lock and listened to the recording, slowed down to half its speed. "Gawd, what a stinker." He listened again, and then a third time, still unable to identify the type.

"No wonder they didn't bother with external security. This is a bloody special patent." He listened again and then replaced the audio sucker onto the lock.

"Hopeless." He put the equipment away, knowing that he would only set off an alarm if he tried to get in.

Once on the ground again he summoned the engineer robot. It was small, built to scramble into difficult and cramped areas for repair.

"Tell me, old son, how do I open the door on this crate?"

"Entry selected." The robot would only have a minimum speech centre.

"Yes, I'm aware of that. I don't want to get into the launch, I just want to open the door so I can have a look."

The robot considered this for a moment, evidently not

having heard such a request before, it had no ready answer. It seemed to be searching for instructions to say "no" but unable to find any it turned and led the way back into the force elevator. They ascended and stood outside the entrance. The robot touched the lock panel and the door slid away. Simple, the correct electronic pattern and anyone could do it. Now came the problem, for the moment Vandal stepped inside, the robot would set off an alarm.

He stood there, looking inside and the robot stood beside him, waiting. Funny things robots, no sense of priority. Sometimes this can be an advantage. With a living guardian Vandal would have been hurried, but with this dum-dum he had all the time he needed to decide what to do next.

"Pretty, ain't it?" He turned toward the robot, seeing it out of the corner of his eye and then he turned back again as though he had just spotted something.

"I say, good gracious me, there's a fault."

"Fault—" The response was emotionless, but registered.

"Yes, look, on the main control console. I can see it from here. There's a quarter light on. On this model that signifies a fuel leak, some evaporation somewhere."

"Evaporation, fuel leak, must remedy." The robot adopted a kind of nervous urgency. The truncated little walking technician turned toward the elevator and then back toward Vandal. It lifted a hand shaped more like a spanner, and was about to say something, but decided not to.

"Go on, old son.I'll stay here and make sure nothing gets worse. You go and have a look at your fuel leak. Mustn't let it get out of hand."

"Fuel leak, mustn't let it get out of hand . . ." The robot left the elevator at the bottom, still muttering. Vandal stepped into the launch, touched the control pattern instructors, fed in flight patterns to the computer and lifted off.

"Hi, we thought you'd never get here." Steeleye, Chaos and Boy teleported on board as the launch broke out of gravity.

"No trouble, such polite robots they have on Bantam.

Nasty moment with the lock device, though. Thought I might not make it."

"Right, now we can travel in comfort for a while." Chaos began to remove her clothes again.

"Goody, goody, who's for a bit of . . . "

"You've had all you're getting. Go and supervise the flight. I don't want any bad driving or wrong turns. Keep your eyes on the road."

Vandal dragged his stunned gaze from Chaos's naked body as she slowly crossed her legs and lay back against the couch.

"O.K. So, who knows the flight instructions for Carosh?" Vandal said – irritated that he had gone to so much trouble for nil reward.

"Just ask the computer," Steeleye said.

"It doesn't . . . " The negative was broken, Vandal never got it out. As he sat, he swivelled his pilot seat to have another look at the naked Chaos. His view was obscured by a line, *the* line, the Sideways Man. For some reason Vandal was speechless. He couldn't get the information across to anyone else, and none of them was watching. The Sideways Man materialised and without a word raised a blaster at Steeleye.

"Christ's alive . . . " Vandal gasped the words out, the only words that would come to him, but they didn't help, for Kimber pressed the contact as Steeleye turned to respond to the sentiment. The blast gutted him, disrupting his entire chest and stomach area, destroying half his body.

Kimber didn't say a word. He coldly dealt the fatal blow, turned into the Wideways and was gone.

Chaos was the first to move. She darted from the couch before Vandal had even closed his mouth, swept him aside and touched off the computer's instructor controls. They went into teleport, then down the Wideways, faster than time itself, with Chaos standing naked, a motionless figurehead on the prow of the ship, clutching at the controls and staring down at the body of Steeleye, more dead than death.

"A ship approaching, in teleport to orbit, unidentifiable. Wait! No, there are familiar bodies on board. Come, send for Tousle."

Steeleye's body was carried from the launch by two Eumigs and placed quickly in Tousle's bio-chamber. The very same bio-chamber that had built Chaos.

"This will take time, Chaos. You had better rest. Take Boy and the vagrant, go to the rest apartment and sleep. I will call you when I have news. There is much damage to the tissue. I shall have to make some replacements. Go now, you will not help me by hovering here. Fear not, there is a good chance that he will live again!

They had teleported across many light years and out of the Wideways from one dimension to another, back to their home planet. Back to the world of Zrost where Tousle the Creature Scientist had built Chaos. The great Eumig race, the mighty Androids who had conceived the Man Steeleye to help them against the Sylva. Now, in time of desperate need Chaos's first thought was to get Steeleye's body back to his fathers and try to repair him before it was too late. She knew that they were the only ones able to help and now all she could do was pace the floor and wait.

She finally managed to persuade Boy to take a hypnotic to make him sleep and sat beside his bed, her eyes glazed, watching the child's troubled dreams and fearing even to think what would become of life if Steeleye were not to recover.

Vandal slumped in a corner of the chamber, tired and shocked, even a little sad. Now there was nothing he could do, or was there?

Chaos did not notice him leave the chamber.

"The vagrant has teleported from the planet."

"Send Timor. Instruct him to observe and help if required. I have a feeling that little fellow might do something foolish."

Vandal knew how carefully timed Steeleye's venture was. He knew that he planned to go to Carosh to speak with the people of Yellow's old race, to find what had happened all those thousands of years before, when the feud first sparked. Now it would be months perhaps before Steeleye could do anything, if ever. So hero Vandal took it upon himself to do the job. He teleported to Carosh. But, being an experienced varg he went via the back door, which in the circumstances turned out to be the best thing he could have done.

He adjusted his arrival to an isolated part of the planet some fifty kilometres from the central planetary city. It was called Carosh, as was the planet. There was no class system on Carosh, no privilege structure. The people either lived in the city or the country and swapped work and abodes at will. A neat system. Anyone living in the city could arrange a house swop with anyone living in the country, and vice versa. Jobs, too, were interchangeable as they all worked in the underground mines.

As Vandal arrived he did not notice the tall robot Timor slip behind a block of subterranean chutes and escalators.

"Well, here we are Vandal, me old son, now what?"

He had chosen to come to Carosh at a time soon after Yellow's departure, using the Wideways contact that Steeleye had set up from the castle on the Crystal Planet.

"Quiet little place. Not much use to a varg. Still, we have an errand to perform." He set off toward the city, using a small directional device borrowed from the launch in which they had travelled to Zrost.

Timor followed silently and unseen, close behind.

The terrain was completely flat, marbled with unreclaimed marshes and uncultivated grassland. Here and there, at four or five hundred metre intervals there were small elaborate plastic structures in a variety of odd shapes that appeared to have sprouted like mutant mushrooms out of the ground. None of them had its own patch of land, no fencing or ditching, no natural boundaries. There was no sign of any living creature. A fine soft wind blew across Vandal's face. He shivered as he gazed across the bleak landscape. He set his body jet pack to a slow, hovering level and allowed it to carry him gently through the air about twenty metres off the ground.

This made life difficult for Timor as Vandal could see most of the ground below him. Timor waited until he was well away and, using a telescopic lens to track him, he lifted to one hundred metres above ground and followed.

Within minutes they were approaching the outskirts of the city.

Vandal was getting too close now for comfort and he decided it was time to drop down onto the surface and do a bit of walking, a method of travel familiar to most vargs and to Vandal in particular.

"Should have brought my walking togs with me," he muttered to himself. The plan he had was largely unplanned and the hope fairly vain that somehow he would be able to get through to a central government where he might seek audience with a leader of some kind. He had not the slightest knowledge of Yellow's race, and even less idea of what link, if any, Yellow maintained with them. But the vargs were accustomed to ignorance in such matters. They never expected to be welcome anywhere and Vandal was ready for a difficult time on Carosh.

Timor dropped lower, ready for action. But he was suprised by Vandal's dexterity. His body was agile and fit and whenever anything moved before him his keen sight anticipated it.

Timor, watching from the air, felt he was tracking a nervous bird, flitting through a jungle, avoiding anything that moved. And his progress was rapid. Soon they had entered a busy and crowded area with many of Yellow's race going about their business. They did not see, or if they did, they did not notice, Vandal, as he slipped quietly and efficiently between them and their homes. Vandal, like all those of his kind, had developed a skill for finding a way around places that were totally unfamiliar. It wasn't a matter, simply, of the language being different, like travelling as a visitor to a foreign country. The whole atmosphere and way of life was alien. There were no points of reference, no signposts, no ways in which he could set his mental compass to find what he looked for. Steeleye would have gone straight for the largest and most central building, but

Vandal had chosen to search his way through the peripheries.

Eventually, he came to a permanent structure. It was built from toughened plastic and stood high above the surrounding city.

"Well now, I wonder if this is the big boy's house or a public lavatory?"

There were no roads and no forms of ground transport, so that the method of travel was a mystery.

Everyone looked like Yellow. They all wore long, loose-fitting robes of various colours and their hair was varying shades of gold, from the floss that haloed the children to the grizzled locks of the old. A few people had flashes of other colours on their breasts and there was a variation in physical appearance. Vandal presumed these must be two sexes, although with all similarly dressed, it was hard to tell them apart.

He approached the tall building, people were coming and going freely.

"Doesn't smell like a lavatory, but then maybe a Pierrot's pee is odourless." He snickered to himself and stored that one away for future rhyme.

Up the steps, unnoticed through the front door.

"Cosy!" he mumbled. "I wonder if they speak the lingo?"

"I say, old boy," he went up to an official standing by the door, "is this where I get my card stamped?"

He turned to Vandal and his face took on a kind of smile as his arm stretched from under his cape and pointed into the building.

"Thanks, old son, nice of you to offer." And in he went.

There were doors to the left of him and doors to the right, each one bearing unfathomable signs. He knocked on the first and got a silent response. So he opened it.

"Anybody at home?" His voice croaked. Inside there were about ten "Yellows," all alike and all involved in some kind of conference, their shoulders bent and their heads close together.

"Sorry to interrupt your scrummage, lads, but I was wondering whether . . . "

"Next office," came a sharp, quite unexpected response from one of the gathering, barely turning from his purpose, whatever it might have been. It looked slightly sinister to Vandal.

"Maybe that's how they get their babies," he muttered as he left the room, thinking vaguely that it was fortunate they spoke his Univerlinguous, but not questioning why. The next door was the same as the last and Vandal knocked again. Getting no response as before, he entered. In this room the appearance was similar to a social gratis office where they hand out free food, bedding and a credit or two for the next day. There were five or six "Yellows" sitting behind desks with nothing at all in front of them, twiddling their middle fingers. When Vandal stuck his head round the door they smiled in unison and practically mesmerised him with their egg-shaped eyes.

"Hello, my name's Vandal. I would like to see the King please."

"Sit down, Vandal. We'll see what can be arranged."

Vandal frowned. He had had some easy times. He had had some very easy times. He had even had such easy times that he had wondered at those times whether he would ever get out alive. In his experience ease in getting something you wanted meant that someone else wanted you to get it, and therefore wanted something in return that you invariably did not want to give, like your life for example. He had had some easy times, but this was bloody ridiculous. He turned around and jumped, for sitting behind him in one of the waiting seats was a huge robot.

"Watcha," he said to the robot who did not respond.

He knew it was a Eumig and he felt relieved to see him, but at the same time uneasy, for in his experience robots meant nothing but trouble.

The smiling circle of "Yellows" said in sing-song unison, "It has been arranged. You can see the King in three points."

"Ah, good, yes, thank you, er, where shall I wait?"

"Right here."

"Thank you. I'll sit with my friend."

Vandal got up and parked himself next to the robot who shifted along a bit as if to say he wasn't supposed to know he was there.

"Too late now, old son. I've just told them you're my friend. You are my friend, aren't you?"

"My name is Timor. I was sent to keep an eye on you."

"Is your eye like Steeleye's eye?"

"Both my eyes are like Steeleye's eye."

"Can you blow the hell out of anything as Steeleye can?"

"Should I wish to, yes."

"Can you smile?"

"Why should I wish to smile? I can express pleasure, should I wish it, through my emotion simulators."

"Can you screw?"

"Please don't ask stupid questions or I'll leave you here on your own."

"I see. Well that establishes the friendship bit anyway." They sat in silence.

"The pee of a Pierrot is pure,
There ain't not a pong, to be sure,
You can tell 'em apart
By the fact that their fart
Is as easy as crom to endure."

The robot Timor remained unimpressed.

"Have you heard the one about the Hapidilc?"

"What is a Hapidilc?"

"Very stupid. There was this Hapidilc you see, in Baramour."

"Where's Baramour?"

"Oh, you're no fun you aren't. How can I tell you a joke about a Hapidilc on Baramour if you don't know what a Hapidilc is and you don't know where Baramour is?"

The robot gave Vandal a tolerant sideways look and resumed his uncommitted position.

Vandal twiddled his thumbs and gave up the unequal battle.

"Would you come this way please. You may bring your friend too."

They were both led past the desks and through another office and into a corridor.

"The King is presently indisposed and has asked you kindly to speak to his assistant."

"Having his supper eh?" Vandal offered.

"You are most gracious."

"Yes, I would have said so. Nice of you to observe."

They were led finally into a poky little office off the corridor. Inside sat a "Yellow," very delicate, clean and neat, upright, behind a small desk. He had the mien of a clerk and rubbed his hands gently together as though each needed the reassurance of the other.

"Please sit. My name is Hapidilc."

"Dear oh dear," muttered Vandal to Timor.

"Illogical," was the doubtful response.

"You have made some request about having a card stamped. If you would be kind enough to produce it, I will stamp it."

"Oh, er, yes, that's er very kind. Well, we had another matter of greater urgency. Perhaps the card stamping could wait until a little later."

"Certainly, as you wish."

"It's in connection with a shipment of crom."

"Oh, yes, a shipment of crom. Er, where was the shipment due to go and when?" Hapidilc seemed to have the matter under his control already, his finger hovering above a control on the viseo beside the desk.

"Yes, well, that's the point. It was never delivered you see. It was due to go to er, um, Aspu. I made the order myself with one of your colleagues, some time ago. I haven't been able to get back here for some while and I wondered what happened to the shipment."

"Who was the order taken by?"

"I don't remember precisely but I know it was done on

the authority of someone else by the name of Pink, or Blue or . . . "

"Uh, Yellow?" Hapidilc suggested the name slowly.

"Yes, that was it, Yellow. I knew it was one of the spectrum waves."

"Indeed, would you be kind enough to wait here, and I'll check the order details. I won't keep you long."

The clerk departed.

"What was all that about?" Timor asked, aghast at Vandal's nerve.

"Well, I didn't want them to know our connection, did I?"

"But what was all that about crom?"

"Well, you know, we might just get a free load of the stuff mightn't we, you never know your luck."

Hapidilc popped his head round the door.

"Had you, er, paid for the shipment?"

"Oh yes, in cash credits, paid in full."

"Thank you, won't keep you long."

"If I may use the colloquial terms, you've got a nerve."

"Yes, I suppose I have. Keep your stubby fingers crossed old son. We might make it yet."

"In the light of your deviousness I am keeping my fingers occupied otherwise, more in the direction of a neat little laser."

"Hm, never did have much confidence in the living, you robots, did you?"

"Time teaches."

The clerk returned.

"Would you be kind enough to come with me please?"

"Oh, er yes, is there some problem?"

"None whatever, we merely need to establish your order co-ordinates on our computered shipment programmer."

"Ah, oh dear. That might be difficult."

"Could you explain?" He turned and faced Vandal, his smile soured slightly.

"Well, I cannot recall ever making a computered shipment recording. The whole thing was done by sub-space."

"I see, well in that case there should be a sub-space indent on the computer. Come and we'll check."

"Oh, yes, of course."

Hapidilc, evidently not at all stupid, led Vandal and Timor out of the chamber into the corridor again and along a few doors.

"Perhaps you had better go and have a look at our launch, Timor. I have a feeling it needs a bit of juice." Vandal nudged the robot and rubbed his elbow.

"Did you come by launch? Straight into the city?"

"Er, no. We er, miscalculated and landed some fifty kilometres outside town actually, why?"

"It's a good job you did. All launches are caught by the tractor beams over the city and sometimes they never make it past them. We discourage casual visitors and if you don't know our ways you can burn up."

"Thanks for the advice. I'll remember that in future."

"I'm surprised you didn't already know it. Most who do business with us are informed."

"Yes. I have some vague memory of being told at some stage, but your Yellow seemed rather vague about it all."

Timor took Vandal's hint and left the building. Meanwhile Vandal was led into a chamber off the corridor and once inside the door was secured.

"Please sit down." The please was not so much polite, rather more of a threat.

"What's wrong?"

"We would like to know more of your contact with Yellow, and why you have lied about a shipment of crom"

"Oh dear."

Timor moved swiftly once outside the building, jetting himself over the structures out to where they had arrived. Here he stopped and awaited darkness. He had placed a small transmitter on Vandal's clothing. It was small enough not to be noticed but powerful enough to give him a full transmission of the proceedings as they continued.

"I would be grateful to know exactly why you are here on Carosh, from where you have come and any other details that we should know."

"I don't quite follow."

"Please do not treat us like imbeciles. We know that you have lied and we would prefer the truth. Quickly, I have much to do."

"Hm, well, you see, my greatest problem is that . . . oh I can't. I really can't. You'll be furious and beat me up or something."

"We are not in the habit of beating people up. We simply eliminate them if they don't tell us what we want to know."

"I say, that's a bit rough, old boy. Don't you believe in penal rehabilitation?"

"No."

No messing with these boys, thought Vandal.

"I'm . . . I'm . . . a, oh dear. You'll think me so awful."

"Quickly."

"Alright, here we go. I'm a cromoholic and I made the whole thing up to get a free shipment of crom out of you."

"Why did you mention Yellow?"

"I didn't, you did. I simply chose a perfectly normal name type, there are lots of people with colour names on my planet."

"Strange coincidence."

"Very, but then fiction is stranger than fact isn't it? It's all a pack of lies."

"I'm aware of that. The problem that I face is which lie to choose."

"Ha ha, you're quite a joker when you get going aren't you? Have you heard the one about the Shipeldilic on Baramour."

"Please don't fool with me. Let's start again."

"Yes, let's."

"What is your name?"

"Albert."

"Albert what?"

"Albert Tatlock."

"A-l-b-e-r-t-t-a-t-l-o-c-k. And where are you from?"

"Coronation Street."

"Where is Coronation Street?"

"On a planet called Drudgery."

"D-r-u-d-g-e-r-y. Right, now we're getting somewhere."
"Are we? Oh good."
"Why did you come here?"
"For to swizzle you out of a barrel of crom."
"And there are lots of people on Drudgery with colour names?"
"Yes."
"But not you?"
"Oh yes, I forgot, or rather I try to hide it. I've got a middle name you see, another name between the two you wrote down."
"Tell me."
"Must I?"
"Yes, it's very important."
"Very well . . . " Vandal steeled himself, turning his head this way and that to see if anyone was listening.
"Can't you send that lot out?"
"Why?"
"Well, if you had a middle name like mine, you'd want to keep it secret too."
"Stop fooling and give me your name."
"Puce." Vandal shrank into himself in mock-embarrassment.
"Albert Puce Tatlock. Now are you a registered chromoholic?"
"Oh yes, of course, on my planet."
"Then how did you get the launch to come here?"
"Borrowed it off a friend, the robot came with it."
"That's no ordinary robot. That's an Android and judging by its responses a very sophisticated Android. In fact I'd go so far as to say I have never seen an Android like it."
"And you'd be right," Vandal whispered behind his hand and Hapidilc leaned forward. "He's an experimental model, quite harmless you understand, except if you hold me for too long."
"Oh, and what will he do if we hold you for too long?"
"Well, you see," Vandal continued the secretive charade,

"if I am away from him for more than half an hour or so he goes berserk."

"What does that involve?"

"He has a new experimental weapon. His eyes you see, they're actually rather powerful blasters."

"How powerful?"

"Well, I've seen him wipe out a battle launch with one blink and rumour has it that if you put a city round about his sweeping gaze, he could clear the ground for you in a matter of minutes. Now that may be idle gossip but I wouldn't like to be around when they test it."

"No, well, we'll have to do something about that."

"Will we? What?"

"We'll have to let you go, won't we?"

"Yes, well that would seem like an excellent idea. Why don't you do that? After all I've been here a good twenty minutes now."

"Just one more question."

"What's that?"

"When did you last see Kimber?"

"Oh, last wee . . . "

"Take him, put him away somewhere safe. We wouldn't want this resourceful little fellow to get into the wrong hands. And when he's safe and sound go and deal with that robot."

"Fucked that up, didn't I?" Vandal was heard to say as they led him to the dungeons.

"I knew it. Stupid little half-wit." Timor stomped about on the dry, sandy ground, his huge boots kicking up the dust.

He knew that within a matter of minutes they would be out there after him. Either he would have to stand and fight or disappear for a suitable period and return when things had quietened down. "Needless slaughter is not encouraged." Timor mumbled the Eumig primary ruling and took the latter choice. Within seconds of teleporting away, fifteen heavy-duty robots arrived where he had been.

He departed a safe distance and put himself into orbit around Carosh, still picking up Vandal's chatter.

"Now look here, what is all this? What do you think I am? A bit of rubbish just to be thrown onto a garbage dump?"

"More or less, get in there."

"I see."

"What is your name?"

"I've told you, Elsie Tanner."

"That is not what you told me."

"Oh, sorry, I've forgotten which one it was now."

"You're a fool. All we can do now is kill you."

"Then why don't you? Why are you keeping me here? Who told you to keep me here? I demand my rights. I demand as an American citizen. Where's the Ambassador, where's the King?"

"We would be most interested to know where you gather the information with which to lie to us so glibly. Who is Albert Tatlock, where is Coronation Street, what is America?"

"Television I think they used to call it. Yes, television."

Timor decided from listening to this conversation that they had their work cut out in trying to decipher anything coming from the mad mouth of Vandal, so he slipped back into the atmosphere again and made for what looked most like the planet's reception units. There were two guards around the building but no other form of security. Timor neutralised both guards with one glance of his eye and moved silently through one of the entrances. Inside he found various computer banks. Each form of communication had its own computed system, one for sub-space, one for radio wave, one for TI and a fourth one that Timor could not quite make out. It was entitled INTER-DIMENSIONAL RECEPTION. Timor examined the latest message sheets. They were copious, and in some kind of coded language.

There was no one around the area, indeed no one in the building according to Timor's detectors, so he studied the code with his deciphering mechanisms and after much care managed to make some sense of a few words.

" . . . send ten Codas . . . Wideways . . . castle."

That was all he needed. He photographed the message sheet and set off out of the building only to be faced by the heavy-duty robots. Fifteen of them. They must have sniffed the air and detected his arrival.

Timor had been selected by Ifon to go after Vandal for one very good reason. He was one of the most agile of the intelligent Eumig Androids. His body had been built for fighting. His mental capacities were specialist, directed towards the skills of battle and he knew what he was at in a fight. The two eyes, given to all Eumigs, could move independently and to watch a warring Android firing with both eyes swivelling them in every direction, is like watching a cross-eyed lunatic darting about in a fit. The best advice is never to be within range.

Timor took on the first four robots and splattered them across the air as he moved down the line of fire. He rolled, like a western gunman and popped the seams loose down the side of another robot.

They were all firing wildly, but more or less in his direction.

Not efficient robots. He dived low and took the ankles off another two robots. Then much to their chagrin he stood up carrying them both, one in each hand, lifted their bodies high in the air and dashed them down onto two more. As he hurled them he fired with both eyes at a further two. That left four still intact. Timor opened his eyes to full aperture and sprayed a wall of blaster fire in front of him. He closed one eye down to see what the other was up to. Once the fire had subsided he watched the last robot doing a death dance away from him, its body engulfed in flame. The complex wiring and computered intricacies were bouncing out of it in a fireworks display. One dying attempt at attack was made by a fallen robot.

Timor stepped on its arm and kicked it in the chest, crushing the motor fabrics and putting it out of business.

"Nothing like a good scrap," he muttered, teleporting back to Zrost.

Chapter 8

It was night. The night of Zrost's world; a windswept, cool night that brought shivers to the flesh and creeping, doubtful fears into the mind. Chaos walked alone in the open space between her apartment and Tousle's laboratories, where he had been working throughout on Steeleye's body.

She watched the air playing tricks across her tired eyes. Sleep had come only intermittently since Vandal's departure. Most nights she paced the small area round her temporary home. The only comfort was the effect of Zrost. Like a real home; a place where she felt safe, the only place she had ever felt safe. The great lumbering, powerful Eumigs surrounded her with a sense of care and strength. Nothing could penetrate this haven to do harm to her and Boy.

She remembered the times when Steeleye had taken her and made soft sweet love to her in that apartment. The times when she had walked with him alone through the night and talked of all the wonderful things they would do together; how they would conquer worlds and overcome all. And they had. Their dreams had been fulfilled. Until that dreadful journey and the Sideways Man. She vowed that if Steeleye were not to recover she would spend all her days and nights hunting Kimber and she would kill him or be killed herself.

She found her walk moving towards the labs. The lighting was low inside. Tousle had done all he could for the moment and had gone about other tasks. Like all the Eumigs he needed no sleep.

She entered, using her private access touch and walked through the first rooms to the bio-chamber where Steeleye's body lay still and cold. His steel eye still glinted in the dim light. The eye that had saved them on so many occasions. The other eye was closed, and the appearance of one open, metal eye and the other closed and human was sinister. She shivered as she watched over his body.

The laboratory was untidy, filled with apparatus. In one corner lay the PAL that aided Tousle on his biological reconstructions. It had been de-powered and lay, a still disc, as if recuperating for Tousle's next burst of activity.

Steeleye was naked. His chest cavity was covered with a metallic tent but the remainder of his powerful limbs were bared to her sight and touch. So familiar, though now so forbidding and shadowed, grey with the tincture of death. Chaos stood, watching over her man and as she bent her head to kiss his face she felt the hairs on the back of her neck stand up, suddenly. She turned and instinctively touched one hand upon Steeleye's body and the other to a button on her belt. The control sent a thick, double-layered protective shield around herself and Steeleye and the bio-chamber in which he lay. The shield was not visible and it was impenetrable for long periods to any weapon other than the most powerful laser. As she turned, the ominous thin line appeared before her. It thickened, Chaos was rooted to the spot with fear, unsure of everything now. Soon enough the Sideways Man appeared.

"So, quick thinking, Chaos. Your name belies you, that you should have got him here so fast."

"What do you want?" Chaos counted on Kimber not knowing of the force shield.

"I have heard of the Eumigs and their mighty strength. I knew they were clever but I had no idea that they could bring life to death." He ignored her question.

"They are not far from here. I can call them any time."

"Even a Eumig cannot travel faster than light and it would need such speed to prevent me from destroying you both completely. Presumably they cannot reconstruct a living body from disrupted atoms." He pressed the contact of the hand blaster. The ray hit the shield at Chaos's middle and spread over the protection like a flame licking at asbestos.

"Well, well, well, you really have excelled yourself. I am impressed. The protective woman stands over her man against my attack." He fired again, holding the contact open for what seemed minutes to Chaos who felt the heat through the shield, but the effect was nil. "You cannot stand against me for ever, Chaos. I will burn through your shield eventually. Why prolong the suffering? Eventually you will die. It will be more painful if I have to force you to drop that shield."

"You cannot force me to do anything. I am inside with Steeleye and you are outside."

"I have only to drag you from the chamber, Chaos, and he will be unprotected." He darted towards her, using the full strength of his wiry body to knock her off balance. She tried to grab for the chamber and regenerate the force field but he kicked her body from the side and sent her reeling away across the room. He levelled the blaster at the bio-chamber and would have pressed the contact had it not been for Tousle.

"If you fire that blaster Kimber, I will kill you."

Kimber turned and fired randomly at Tousle's body, missing by some two metres as Tousle dropped to one side. He blasted from one eye and burnt the weapon from Kimber's hand, sending it crashing to the ground.

"Curse you, Eumig." Kimber grabbed Steeleye's body and tried to rip the chest protector from it.

Tousle fired again from the same eye and burnt a clean hole in the right side of the Sideways Man.

"Ahhhh," the agonised scream reverberated through the entire building. Kimber turned, beaten, to face his opponents.

"You have declared war upon the Sideways Man, now not only the family of Steeleye will die but Zrost too. You will never survive the future, Eumig." With these vengeful words Kimber turned sideways into the line, shrinking quickly to a spot and then gone.

"Oh Tousle, thank God you were there."

"It is fortunate that I was. Has he done any harm?"

"No, I had a shield up. He was going to burn Steeleye, disrupt him."

"We shall have to lay more secure protection around him

when there is no one here. I doubt Kimber will be back but there is no harm in being careful. I will put a rejector-shield around this building and another round Steeleye. Come, you must take some sleep, you look wan. We cannot have you breaking down. It can only be a few days now before Steeleye regains consciousness and then a few weeks of convalescence. So, stop your fretting and go to bed."

Chaos did as she was bid and Tousle set up the protectors.

Not so far away Timor had returned to Ifon's offices.

"So the vagrants are in the Wideways on Steeleye's contact, around the castle. And you interpret Yellow's message to Carosh as a plea for help?"

"I do, Ifon."

"How can you be sure that the people of Carosh will send the help?"

"Why would they hold Vandal?"

"Perhaps to get his end of the Yellow/Kimber story."

"That will take them forever."

"Don't be fooled by them, Timor, they are subtle people. They will get everything from Vandal without his even knowing he has told it."

"Should I return and get him out?"

"Yes, I suspect that it would be better if they didn't know. No doubt they will be as greedy for the Wideways power as anyone else."

"Have you news of Steeleye?"

"He will recover, despite the further attempt to destroy him."

"Who?"

"Kimber, but Tousle and Chaos sent him off with a large hole in his back. It will take him time to recover from that. I cannot think why Tousle didn't kill him, but I suppose that old robotic law holds good."

"I will return with Vandal."

"Good, try not to knock out too much of Carosh, Timor, they have their own lives to lead."

"I'll do my best."

Chapter 9

In the castle Yellow was making elaborate preparations. The number of vagrants in the mirrors had swelled to fifty, each one occupying his own corridor, each standing quite still, sombre with intent, awaiting patiently the orders of their adopted leader.

Yellow's seal on the mirrors effectively prevented them from reaching his dimension. However, to make absolutely sure he set up a few nasty surprises to repel any unexpected arrivals.

As he viewed activities in the time chamber, lights signalled an arrival through the Wideways.

"Ah-ha, and about time too." He touched a switch and the door of the Wideways time machine opened.

Inside were ten small crates, square, seamless and made of shiny metal. Yellow took a device from his cloaked smock and beamed a tractor ray at the crates, carrying each one out on force fields and placing them side by side in the corridor. He placed a beam around the lot and manoeuvred them from the warp chamber out into the Cantelevator and down to the main entrance hall where he placed each one beside the next in a neat line. The metal was unbroken all round. He was careful to ensure that the operation be carried out correctly. He stood behind the canisters with a hand console. Before opening them he strapped the console to his wrist and placed a tight field around it. He threw a switch and lifted a small flap on the device. Then pressed a hand control and the strange process of the opening of the Codas began.

A fine seam appeared on the top edge of the first canister and the front and top faces of the box lifted away from the square. This process was repeated in each case until ten boxes stood open. The contents were difficult to discern. The boxes appeared to be thick with tightly packed iron filings. Densely black and ominous, they remained quite static. Then the other three faces above the ground flapped down and all five sides were lifted by a force field and piled neatly upon one another. Yellow manipulated the console without moving position. Then, without reason or warning the first square of filings began to change shape.

It was as though they were subject to a magnetic field that altered and progressed. This army of glossy filings began to shuffle its feet, collecting in denser clusters then dispersing and reforming again. They appeared to have a life of their own, shifting and swirling, as they rounded shape and streamed from the box. Their progress was rapid and with skilful manipulation could have been a great deal faster. The first batch settled in front of their canister base and were followed by each of the other nine. These bases were piled on top of the other box sides, and all were disrupted as Yellow pressed a button on the console.

Then he moved another control switch and the ten piles of filings, known to the people of Carosh as Codas, began to merge into one another. They advanced inwards, continually enmeshing and growing vertically all the time. Yellow stopped them for a moment and then gathered them into a tall statue. It stood about ten metres from the ground, black and glistening, and within a few moments, looked like a sinister replica of Steeleye. They had been programmed like swarming ants upon a hill into this instructed shape and now stood, slightly jagged edged and vibrant with imperceptable movement, but nevertheless distinctly in Steeleye's likeness. And there they remained.

There must have been a million of them, in that statue, incorporated and controlled by a strange power mechanism. Yellow was satisfied and departed into the Cantelevators.

Timor was pretty busy too. Somehow or other he had to get Vandal out of there alive without knocking off too many of the Carosh. They would by now have established a fair conception of a Eumig's capabilities once they discovered the scattered remains of the fifteen robots. There was no question of going in and trying to bluff his way out again.

He went first to the nearest moon from Carosh and there he set up a small atom blaster, built to hurl projectiles far into space. He aimed it directly at the centre of the city of Carosh where Vandal was imprisoned and set it to fire pieces of rock from the moon face. Because of the tractor beams over the city the rocks would burn up and cause a bright flare as they raced towards the surface. They would never reach the ground so, despite the fireworks, no damage would be done.

Next he prepared a mirrored force field that would reflect the incinerating rocks and direct these images towards the area where he wanted to land. As the meteors sped towards the surface they and their reflectors would be enough to dazzle all but the most obstinate troglodyte.

With this diversion in the heavens and with good management and fortune on his side, Timor would be able to get to the prison doors and from there he would simply have to play it by ear. He set the blaster on a timer to give him the moments to cover the distance from the moon to the city limits. Then he set up the mirror field. Once on the planet's surface he crossed to within a few kilometres of the city and waited.

Soon from the sky came a great flashing blast.

"Hm, better than I had expected." He started towards the city centre and as he did so the lights became more intense with each projectile. By the time he got to the prison house there was confusion in the city. Everyone was rushing about looking up at the sky, shouting and gesticulating at the firework display popping and sizzling in their atmosphere. Timor entered the building and walked straight past a guard who did not even see him.

Into the corridors and down some steps to the dungeons.

Here he confronted two further guards whom he spoke to in their own tongue, telling them that there was a magnificent spectacle outside.

They didn't question this strange oversized robot but dashed up the stairs to look. Timor went on down.

"Vandal?"

No response. Timor continued across the long level of prison doors.

"Vandal?"

"Yes, here, is that you Timor?"

"Wait, I will blast the door."

"Make sure you don't blast me too. How the hell did you get in here?"

"Through the front door."

"Ask a silly question."

Timor blew a large hole in the centre of the door and Vandal scampered through.

"Hello, me old buddy, boy am I glad to see you. How do we get out of this hole?"

"Straight up."

"Eh?"

"Hold on to my back. I'll strap you on and cover you with a field. You won't be hurt but there might be quite a force. We'll be moving at a few kilometres a second."

"What, through the roof?"

"Yes, once we get onto the ground floor we go straight out through the top and off across land for a few kilometres, then up through the atmosphere and teleport from there. Ready?"

"I suppose so. Not an exit I would have planned myself but you're the boss in these matters. Tighten the belt."

Timor strapped Vandal onto his huge broad back, where he clung like a monkey, and made his way rapidly up the stairs to the floor above. There was one spot on the ground floor where a glass roof led out to the air, and Timor positioned himself there ready for flight. A guard looked at them with doubt and hesitated long enough not to be shot down. Timor blasted upwards, straight through the plate glass roof and into the air. The flashing was still going on in the sky.

The guard watching Timor's departure gasped, his mouth open, turned to a friend and looked at him stunned. The conversation that followed, if roughly translated, went something like this:

"Wassamadda, Fred?"
"Huh?"
"Whassamada, you get sick?"
"They went through the roof."
"Eh?"
"Through the roof, up there."
"What did, what did, Fred? Whatever yer talkin' about, Fred?"
"Those two, they went through the roof, right straight up through the roof, through the bloody roof, straight up, not even so much as a by your leave or a goodbye, straight up through the roof."
"Have you had a medical recently, Fred?"
"I tell you, it was that robot that was here and the little fella we had down in the cellar, they just left by the roof."
"Let's have a look then, eh Fred?"
The other one, not Fred, took Fred by the arm and led him in a fatherly fashion across the corridor to the glass roof to investigate this ludicrous claim.
"Now Fred, let's have a look at this roo . . . ooof."
"You see, there's a bloody great hole up there, they went straight through the glass. I saw them."
"Are you sure Fred, are you absolutely sure you saw them go up through there? It wasn't a bit of rock or something that dropped down through the glass and made that hole?"
"What do you think I am, barmy?"
"Well, no Fred, of course not. I've known you since you was a boy and I'd never suggest a thing like that, but it does seem a little unlikely now doesn't it? I mean really, that a robot and a prisoner could just take off there through the roof and vanish into thin air? I mean Fred, now come on, how could they have got out of the prison for a start? Those doors are a metre thick."
"Listen, you great dunderheaded nitwit, I don't care about the thickness of the prison doors. I saw the robot and the prisoner take off through that roof and I'm going to raise the alarm."

"Oh now come on, Fred, perhaps we should just check the door downstairs first. You might find he was still there eh?"

"How could he be there if he just went through the roof?"

"Yes I know, Fred, but still, let's check eh?"

"And let them get away . . . ?"

Well of course by this time Timor and Vandal were back on Zrost.

Chapter 10

You might imagine that it is easy to get lost in the Universe. That the size and depth of space makes hide and seek an endless game, but with the spreading of intelligent life into the furthest reaches and also with the increase in the speed of space and time travel, there were few parts of the infinite that could not be reached through some means.

The Sideways Man had made himself many bases in many parts of the Wideways where he could return, or pass by or recuperate and his favourite was a place he called Superna.

Superna had been found by chance. It was a planet with a derelict house, built in an ancient style. With little effort he had put it into good order using the equipment he had brought from the castle on the Crystal Planet. For Kimber it was perfect. He couldn't have chosen a better location; it was as if it had been tailored to his needs, for Superna floated in a black hole. It could not be seen from passing launches and it was undetectable unless you were constantly in time and knew what you were looking for.

Most space travellers kept away from black holes for their properties were unpredictable. Somehow Superna had the right co-ordinates to hang in a warp within the black hole of a novad star and Kimber with his power of the Wideways, could go there at will. There was no other living soul within years and it was here that he chose to escape to nurse the vicious wound inflicted by Tousle.

The place was kept in order in his absence by an all-purpose domestic robot and as the Sideways Man materialised in one of the rooms the robot turned to face him.

"Prepare the bio-chamber, I am hurt."

"Yes, where is the wound?"

"Right shoulder, blaster hole."

Within moments Kimber was lying in the chamber and directing the robot.

"Tissue haemorrhage termination."

"Check."

"Replace deltoid fabric."

"In process."

"Prepare scapula."

"Check, in process."

"Remove damaged scapula."

"Check, dissolved."

"Prepare clavicle replacement."

"In process."

"Nerve fibre tissues."

"Ready."

"Connect through broken areas."

"In process."

"Blood channel seizures, remove and replace."

"Check."

"Dissolve damaged clavicle."

"Check, dissolved."

"Replace."

"Check."

"Complete deltoid replacement and attach to scapula."

"Check, adhesion in process."

"Complete nerve fibre tissues."

"Check complete."

"Blood channels."

"Check complete."

"Muscular adhesion."

"Check complete."

"Set physiotherapeutic habilitation at maximum recovery level."

"Check, working."

"Now leave me, I need sleep."

"Check."

The house stood in open grounds, without fencing or barriers. The natural barriers of time and space sufficed to protect Superna. In the gardens there were huge fruits that grew plentifully on trees that spread across the ground, covering ten metres and rising only three. The fruits were used to make Kimber's favourite potion, a beverage that tasted like pawpaws.

The robot went into the garden to pick the fruits ready for Kimber when he came out of the sleep.

Kimber knew little of the previous owner, who built the house, but occasionally his spectre, or a projection of some kind visited the place. Kimber accepted this, uncharacteristically tolerant, as he saw no harm in the visitations of an old-fashioned, sentimental fellow who would wander through the newly conditioned house, aimlessly burbling at the gentle rehabilitation that Kimber had overseen.

The apparition was always dressed neatly, in the outfit of a race of creatures known as the Calves. They had occupied a portion of a nearby galaxy. This fellow had somehow left a projection of himself behind; Kimber imagined that it might have something to do with the nature of the planet's position in a black hole, for the apparition never spoke or seemed to notice his existence and always walked the same ways through the house, appearing for about two hours every few days.

The only other evidence of his former existence was a plaque in the foundations of the house which bore an inscription in Calvanese stating: "There is no truth, everything is a lie", a strangely pessimistic doctrine, yet one disclaimed by its very words.

Kimber would watch him as he set off on his solitary repetitious tour of the house. The robot would clear well out of the way.

On the first occasion the robot had performed a dance down the corridor in front of him, like a cat running from an unexpected intruder, backing into a corner and firing blast after blast at the spectre, gouging great holes in the walls behind, until Kimber neutralised his power source. For some reason the mechanical robot could not reconcile the immaterialism of the old fellow, it failed to tally with his programming and confused his circuitry, so the reaction had been random fear.

Kimber had done all he could to adjust the electronic

receptors, first to make the robot accept the image as harmless, and when that failed, to try and edit it out altogether. But neither had been successful and the poor robot disappeared into its storage area and wouldn't come out until the house ghost had completed his rounds.

Scientists on Kimbernium had long established that the air and the fabrics round it were capable of storing sound and light waves for millions of years. The projection of them at one time or another would depend generally on the acceptance of the visual receptors in the area. A world existing in a warp was a perfect breeding ground for recorded past images, thus Kimber rationalised this walking apparition to himself, though in fact his diagnosis was far from the truth. Kimber would watch the old fellow. And it was on this very day, after he had slept and the shoulder wound had recovered, that he discovered the truth, or the lie, for in fact the inscription was apt.

The robot came bounding into the rest room where Kimber lay.

"Kimber, come, I have discovered something. Come outside, Kimber."

"What the . . . what have you found?" As he spoke he was up on his feet and out through the door. The robot was not prone to excitement and there had to be something in his discovery.

He was led to the garden, just outside the house and where there had been an inscription denying the viability of truth, there was now a hole. The stone had been swung away.

"I touched the wall, Kimber, here, and the stone moved. I did not enter, I am not programmed for such areas."

"No, quite right. Remain here and I will see what's inside."

As he entered the chamber lit up, suddenly, and he could see that it spread across most of the foundations of the house, and down into the ground, so that the chamber was some three metres high. There were no support struts of any kind and Kimber wondered at having not discovered the hideaway during the time he had used the house.

At the centre of the chamber was a large, square, transparent block; to one side a foot plate with a series of wave touch controls. Kimber approached it and looked at the controls, squatting down to see them better. They were inscribed in Calvanese.

"Get me the translator."

"Check."

Moments later the robot returned and Kimber went to the door and took the small machine that could be used to decipher the language. He beamed it at the inscriptions and it spoke the translation in Univerlinguous.

"Record." One control.

"Playback." Another.

"Erase." A third.

"Adjust record" and "Multi-record".

"Just like an ordinary recording machine."

He passed his hand over the playback control and the robot squawked outside the chamber, scampered off and could not be brought back. The spectre was doing his rounds. Kimber popped out of the chamber and saw the old fellow walking on his usual path.

"So it can be done manually. A straightforward recording." He stopped the playback with a further control marked STOP and looked over the remaining inscriptions.

"Box message record, and box message playback." He touched the box message playback and watched.

Inside the transparent box was the same figure and after adjusting himself comfortably on an invisible seat he spoke:

"I am Conifer. I do not know to whom I am speaking for this message was recorded for posterity. However, this planet is now passing into a black hole and I do not know of any method of preserving matter under such conditions." Kimber kept the translator on reception and the words were passed through to come out in Univerlinguous.

"I have lived here for a long time, in exile from my own planet which is named Calve. It does not matter why I was exiled but what is important is that if this place should by some freak of nature survive the black hole, there is a secret buried which may be of some use to whoever listens to me and whoever watches my image walk through the house.

"Whoever you are, if you are in this place, you must be here to escape from something. For no one troubles to find a lost planet in the centre of a black hole unless he wishes to escape. If your escape is not complete and you need to travel further into the arms of oblivion then there is a passage way here."

Kimber leaned forward closer, Conifer continued.

"The place you will discover is not known to me for I have not been there myself yet. I have some six midiums before I must leave and most of my preparations are complete. This recording is the last before the planet will be sucked into the imploding nova and I must leave before the entire matter is destroyed. Before I give you the exact instructions I would be grateful if you would leave this recording or duplicate it in your own way for any other who might come after you." Conifer smiled as he spoke. "Who knows – my private world may one day be known as the passageway to eternity. I cannot imagine that such a thing is possible but if I have learnt anything in my short life it has been always to deny the truth. For there is no truth, everything changes too fast." He paused again. "Now, if you will attend me well, I will instruct you on the method of your departure. Only be warned, once you have taken this step there is no returning to any life that you have taken now. The door you are about to enter is the end of the Universe . . ."

Chapter 11

At one given point, a moment in time, if such a moment could be found in so diffuse a Universe, there were three worlds, with three people each connected, each primed for an event that was bound to take place.

On Zrost there was Steeleye. On the Crystal Planet was Yellow who awaited events, his defences at the ready; and on Superna there was Kimber, the Sideways Man, preparing his attack and his departure. Three mighty powers and their aids, ready to do battle for the Wide-ways and the secrets of the crossword. The winner of this great prize might inherit the Universe or die in the attempt. Like three slaves of ancient times, captive to their own ambitions, one at each corner of the arena, weapon in hand, ready to do battle.

The first onslaught was characteristic. Knowing nothing of the others' intentions, both Steeleye and his band and the Sideways Man were headed directly to the source of the prize, the Crystal Planet. And so began a fight to be cherished in the history of all time.

Inside the hall, the vast entrance to the castle of the Crystal Planet, there stood only the Codas statue of Steel-eye. Yellow was not to be seen and silence settled lazily over the high-walled castle. The air cleaved without a sound; the ominous straight line quivered like a lethal arrow extending two metres from the ground. Its movement diminished to a waver, its thickness still doubtful, and then decisively it swelled as always into the shape of a tall, slim, powerful man, head turning this way and that. Kimber had been watching the castle from the Wide-ways Alley for a while before appearing. He knew of all that had happened, he had done his research well before bursting silently into the old castle built so many thousands of years before. He knew of Steeleye's gentle recovery at the hands of the Eumigs, he knew of the vargs and of some, though not all, of Yellow's plans.

From the Wideways Alley he had watched the strange tall Steeleye statue standing in the entrance hall and felt irrational concern at it. It did not fit with the relationship that he knew had now developed between Yellow and Steeleye. Why should Yellow have a statue built to Steeleye? But the thing looked harmless enough and Kimber had never met, in all his travels, the terrors of the Codas.

He looked about him and moved away from the stairwell toward the door of the castle, checking the immediate entrance. He returned and glided silently up the stairs like a raven within the castle. He did not use the Cant-elevators, for he knew that Yellow would have them monitored. His tall beaked figure vanished into the darkness.

Moments later another shadow appeared between the two mirrors of the corridor and expanded into Steeleye. His image was unreflected in the mirrors for he had chosen to remain in the Alley of the Wideways. He looked upon his friends the vargs who looked back at him without seeing. He stepped out of the Alley and his reflection appeared through the millions of Wideways either side of him. He took a small device from his belt and neutralised the force field that prevented the vargs from moving through the Wideways into the castle.

One by one they stepped like images from a nightmare through the mirrored corridors into the castle.

As simply as they might step through open doors the fifty vargs executed one of the most complex time travel motions, moving, some of them, through over twenty dimensions, across twenty totally separate universes into the castle until they were all assembled.

They did not wait for orders from Steeleye, for their tasks were pre-arranged and each one, upon entering the same dimension, moved off at a fast pace to their allotted positions in the castle.

Chaos had her own task to perform and stayed carefully out of sight, watching all that came together.

Steeleye remained, like a benign captain covering his crew until all were within and then moved away and up into the Cantelevator that led to the museum chamber. He was unhindered in his quest until he arrived.

"You might be advised to remain where you are, Steeleye, though I doubt you will heed such advice, but I am well hidden and have monitors scattered around the castle. You are, I believe, far from alone, but there are those here about which you do not know. Kimber is lurking in some distant part and friends of mine are prepared. Your faithful helpers will not be much use to you for I know where they are all hidden, they will not move far now without suffering some unpleasant end. However, for you I have a special gift. I felt that as you suffer so mighty a reputation I should pay a tribute. I have had a statue built in your commemoration. I thought it only fair to leave some replica of your coming when we are all gone from this forsaken place. It stands in the hallway and I would grant you a look at it before you die. Though I believe you have died once already, Steeleye. My felicitations, I trust you do not subscribe to the idea of more than two lives, you may be disappointed."

"I imagine you have learnt the answer to your final question on the crossword, Yellow?"

"I will learn that when I have disposed of you and our mutual aggressor. I don't think the vargs you have brought will be too difficult to persuade to my way of thinking and I believe it is they who hold the scientomagic power to release the secret of the Tetrahecular."

"That is correct. I wish you good fortune, Yellow."

As he spoke he caught a brief glimpse of the Sideways Man in the spot he had last appeared 7,000 years before, perched high on the podium above the museum chamber.

"Kimber, I see you, like an evil bird, you perch on your death post, waiting for your prey," Yellow shouted through the hidden channels in the museum. "But I am not here to be blasted this time. You cannot get me, you cannot get me . . ." Yellow chanted a childish song at the Sideways Man in defiance of his power. But Kimber remained silent.

Steeleye moved to the stair-well and walked slowly down through the castle, passing the various lost levels, like the lord he was determined to become.

They were like three wrestlers, each one unwilling to declare the fight begun, each one assessing the others' intentions, but none quite sure enough to set the battle in motion.

Everything remained silent for some while and then a dim flash occurred within the castle, a twist of position, as though a light source had fused, or the foundations of the planet had taken a turn and developed a fault. A small rumble rippled across the whole fabric of the castle and Yellow let out a loud curse.

"What are you at, Kimber? What game do you play now? Can you not learn that this castle is mine? I claim it for my own. Release your secret, Kimber, and be gone, you cannot remain here. You are an intruder in the realms of Yellow."

No word.

"Listen to me, Yellow, and you too, Kimber." Steeleye stood in the entrance hall and spoke in a low voice.

"I have an accomplice. At this moment she stands on the moon of the Crystal Planet. There she holds greater power than any of us. The power of the warp, Yellow. She has turned the 5D time stream away from the time chamber and onto the entire castle. We are now in Time gentlemen, all of us, and everything around us."

"What foolishness is this, Steeleye?"

"No foolishness, Yellow, but good sense, my friend. If she wishes she can curtail the power of the castle in Time and send us all to oblivion, on a journey that will last forever. Should you stand outside the castle you will see that it has gone, that we are not here but in no time, no time for ever."

"Curse you, Steeleye, you will suffer now."

As Steeleye stood in the entrance hall he turned to see

the statue beside him change shape. It moved as though by a corporate will of its own. What was his likeness before degraded into a seething amorphous stream of black intent.

There could be no question that it bore malice, a sense of real malevolence was directed at whomsoever stood within its path in that muddled time.

It reared up like a charmed snake uncoiling from a basket, altering yet again into a flat river of danger and horror. It stalked Steeleye, as a powerful force will stalk its victim in confidence of the kill. Like a serpent before a vole, summoning its venom, like a shark circling the failing swimmer, it prolonged the terror it engendered. But if these deadly Codas had intelligence they underestimated the power of their opponent.

"Prepare for your death, Steeleye, life and good fortune have evaded you this never-day."

Yellow spoke the words like a lord and master exacting punishment on a wayward servant but even Yellow knew nothing of the fearless power that lay dormant in the body of the Eumigs' creation.

Steeleye let fly a blast from his eye and shivered the length of the Codas before him, heating their body of metal, throwing in his own test of strength; a simple gesture to show his quarry that they would best prepare more carefully the death strike they wished to inflict.

The Codas snatched at Steeleye, overreaching to a metre behind him, overbalancing and wavering the full length of their steely tension.

Steeleye blasted again at the weakest point of the arm, projecting through twenty metres beside him. The length snapped and one part fell, scattering its million parts like black pins. The move gave him no advantage, for the severed part reassembled into a spearhead and took on a separate life, launching an attack from flank and front. Steeleye jumped, lifting his agile body ten metres into the air and over the back section that now spread like a dreadful contagion about his feet.

He blasted again at the cancerous carpet of fine metal

filings which seethed and slid below him, this time with much greater power, but the blast of energy only sufficed to fire them to greater and faster movement. The area that had taken the brunt of the heat turned dull red and shot more rapidly across the floor toward Steeleye's ankles, dashing about them like ants ready to plunder a giant food store.

Steeleye did not contemplate their power, did not imagine what would become of him should their morbidity enter his body for the spread of them seemed as inexorable as a tidal wave. By now the other part had mustered for the attack. Like minute battalions they set together, rank upon rank, a million of them amassing before him. His defences were not effective against them but to test their strength to the full he put his eye to its maximum power and sent out a blast which shored up the ground from under them, scattering their numbers into the gaping craters. The blast was so strong that their corporate identity seemed to have been dispersed too, they drew back to consider their position and synchronise their attack, but their number had not diminished. They were unharmed, fizzing with heat yet tight with tenacity and purpose, slightly disrupted but little more. The ground was badly damaged and Steeleye noticed one unexpected factor. Where he had fired his eye to the ground there was a huge hole, some four metres across, but in one part the beam had done no damage. The Tetrahecular was intact. The great circle that surrounded the strange complex mathematical diagrams had been directly in his line of fire and yet it remained complete. And more still, in the glance of his human eye he had seen that the Codas did not advance onto the design. They circled it, avoiding the area as though it were taboo or carried some power they could not encompass.

Again they amassed, this time rearing up to Steeleye's height as though to knock him off his feet. He blasted again, a full blast ranged directly at the centre of their stand, but the blast hit and knocked away one portion, merely displacing it. The top and bottom parts enmeshed, dropping upon one another replacing the dislodged section. The bulk simply thinned slightly and soon enough the piece knocked from the centre recovered and joined the ranks at their back once again, thickening the battering ram.

He was not getting any further and without thought he stepped smartly into the Tetrahecular.

Though it brought him closer to them, he felt instinctively that there was some unknown safety in that magic circle. He had not stepped there before, and realised that during the attack they had been forcing him away from the Tetrahecular.

As he stepped in, they reared back. Like a huge whiplash they curled, wavered, and hung in the air, circling round the Tetrahecular surrounding every part of the circle building up a wall as high as Steeleye's generous head. They could neither move into the circle nor could they move over it so they did the next best thing. They confined Steeleye within it.

A jolt of panic shot through Steeleye as he realised their intentions. He could not be reached by them but they were making it impossible for him ever to get out.

A feeling of claustrophobia overcame him, the tight attack was cutting his air, too close for comfort for the circle could only have been a couple of metres in diameter and although he knew they could not reach or touch him, there was always the fear that he would make a wrong step or put out a hand in panic and they would grab a limb and drag him from the circle. There was no doubt that their combined strength was greater than his and that their lethal power was that of suffocation. They would grab him and simply cover his body with their mass, entering every crevice and orifice and filling his lungs until he ceased to breathe.

It was that fate or remain where he was until help came. He could not afford to be left there, the others needed his leadership, his aid, for the plan to work. There had to be a way. He pressed the button on his belt and, without warning, shot high into the air, thrusting up, still within the protective confines of the circle but up and up. The Codas were fast to react, indeed their movement seemed almost to anticipate Steeleye's so that the tunnel they had begun increased in height with their quarry, up and up.

As Steeleye went so he recorded in his mind the height that he climbed. Twenty metres, thirty, forty, fifty, the ceiling seemed to reach to the sky. They were fifty-five metres from the ground now and still a little way to go. He watched the tunnel coming up with him and noticed that although there were at least a million of them they were thinning, as they increased their range and consequently lessened their tension. They could not afford to withdraw their coverage at any level for Steeleye's body moved too fast to allow any exit points. They were attempting to cover every inch of space between the floor and the ceiling.

The Codas were so thinly spread now that light was penetrating. But still no air, or not enough for Steeleye's gasping body. The exertion of the fight had tired him, his heart pounded and his lungs ached with the lack of oxygen. Within a fifty-eight metre tube he was completely confined, from floor to ceiling. Two metres in diameter and perfectly circular, he had created his own coffin.

"A handsome sarcophagus, Steeleye, worthy of you. You have fought a fine battle, now meet your makers, if the Eumigs occupy hell. Go, Steeleye, give up the fight, for the Codas will remain there until every breath is shed from your mighty bo—" But the words were not complete from Yellow's lips as he saw Steeleye or rather a massive blast of heat and light burst from the tubular tomb.

Again his aggressors had underestimated the Lord of Space. He knew the walls of his prison had grown thin and he knew his own thrust power. With every ounce of strength and instantaneous power he had thrust his body backwards, using eye blast and the small jets on his feet. The view from the outside was remarkable for at first there was a great bulge suddenly to one side. The thrust from his body pushed the wall out and then directly opposite the structure bent and crashed outwards, the bulging side bursting forth.

From the hole came a huge, curved figure smashing through. The image was blurred and sudden, but it torpedoed like a man falling from an enormous height into water, seen from below the surface. The force with which Steeleye continued his flight was great enough to prevent the Codas from grasping his body. Their tenacity was astonishing for, although forcefully dispersed and with the thinnest skin, they wrapped themselves about the human cannonball. But Steeleye had covered himself in a force field as he went and using the field he generated an electric current setting up a reverse pole magnetic force which threw the metallic Codas from their prey.

But the chase was not over yet. There was to be no rest for Steeleye. The Codas were tireless and like a swarm of vengeful bees they gathered themselves up, unable to fly through the air they earthed themselves by the smallest chain to the ground and formed a dense pyramid of strike power.

Instinctively Steeleye made for the door of the castle, realising in the split second that the entire structure of the castle was in warp. Exit from it might deprive him of either his physical stability or his sanity or both. But there was no choice. He could not remain in there, not with those killers so hard on his heels.

The open door of the castle was before him and he knew that to go from a balanced warp out into timelessness was not only dangerous but unpleasant. The barrier of the door was there before him as he moved at nearly twenty metres a second. Watched by Yellow and now by Kimber, Steeleye's body was seen to enter the timeless outside, vanishing into nothing, the Codas right behind, then silence.

Yellow did not believe that Steeleye could survive the change in time that would have thundered upon him with awful suddenness but knowing of his powers of recovery, he sent forward a mounted blaster to stand at the entrance to the castle in case the unpredictable man should by some fluke return. It was set to blow anything that entered to kingdom come. One second after it was in place, about fifteen seconds after Steeleye and the Codas had left, Steeleye's figure reappeared at the entrance and the blaster let fly at full power. The heat and light thrown out smacked against the time interlude at the door and threw up a panel of whiteness and flame, engulfing the figure that stood in its deadly path. But once the shot had ceased and the light waves stopped their nauseous confusion, Steeleye stood unharmed, untouched. He was quite still, there was no sign of the Codas nor remarkably of damage to his body.

The blaster fired again and the performance was repeated, leaving the huge, tall body still intact, not a bruise or abrasion, not a heat mark or any other visible signs of the holocaust he had survived.

"Are you a god, Steeleye? Are you a confounded god, what are you that you can withstand death with such ease?" Yellow hurled the words out of the unseen speakers about the hall so that the power of his voice cursed the very air that surrounded them. He was desperate, teeth gritted, furious that no weapon he possessed seemed able to repulse his foe.

"Now you will credit my reputation, Yellow, after all it was you who brought me here on the strength of it, was it not?"

The voice did not issue from the figure standing at the door.

Yellow looked at the screens in front of him as he stood in the hidden viewer room. His eyes moved from one to another, his hands swiftly from control to control, lighting up every monitor in the building; searching for Steeleye. But there was no sign, not at first. No shadow, nothing. Then there was a movement, a rapid shift of shadows across a dimly lit stone wall. Yellow touched a contact and a blaster secreted in the wall fired a shot and hit the wall where the shadow had left no mark. Then in another screen, far from the first, a figure skittled across the screen and again Yellow fired, but missed. Then another and another until they were like flannel-footed thieves tripping at angles through the castle so fast that Yellow could not catch them at all, and fired crazily at anything and everything.

"These are my friends, Yellow, don't hurt them will you?" And more rushed across the monitors to be missed by Yellow.

"Look out, here comes another, fire, Yellow, fire, quick, you'll never catch them, they're too fast and too many, Yellow. Quick, keep firing." The blasts reverberated through the castle in every small corridor and corner.

"Can't catch us, can't catch us, catch us, catch us . . ."

The unison of vagrant voices taunted Yellow from the screens and then there was stillness. Yellow watched the monitors, trying to anticipate the next move, but what he saw he would not believe, for every single screen showed a cloaked figure, at the same exact moment fifty vargs stood out from a corner and remained still.

Yellow did not fire. He didn't know which one to begin with, and he fingered the fire buttons but pressed none of them. As he floundered they performed their second movement, again exactly timed.

They threw back their cloaks, unloading their tall bodies. Yellow gasped. They were all exactly the same, without variation, they were precise in every detail. Every one was Steeleye.

"Kill me now, Yellow, I am unprotected, all of me." And Steeleye, all the Steeleyes, laughed, the echoes, loading the air of the castle billowing in upon Yellow in his small hide hole.

Yellow pressed the fire buttons, one after another and as he did so a Steeleye would drop to the ground and immediately be replaced by another. And another and another.

A rippling scream reverberated across the speaker system.

"You will keep your reputation, Steeleye, you will keep

it, for I will go mad . . ." The blasting stopped and there was silence.

All the figures and duplicates of Steeleye vanished instantly.

Chaos had watched the whole act from the point when she played her unexpected part. As Steeleye had burst from the cylinder of the Codas she had constructed a temporal field outside the door of the castle. She knew what Steeleye had planned, for his TI delivery was profound in the fear of the moment and from her grandstand seat on Tristor she could follow his moves. As he burst from the door she caught him neatly in the time net and whisked it away before the Codas exited. Held in the bubble he was carried up above the level of the door and the Codas plunged straight into the timeless void outside the castle to be dissipated, scattered across forever.

Steeleye had taken advantage of the time properties in which he was now floating. He had released himself from the temporal field and into the emptiness where the time duplications were endlessly available to him. He knew that if he projected them into the castle they would only last for a short while but it would add to the confusion and give him time to find either Yellow or Kimber.

He instructed the vargs through small receivers to play hide and seek and then stand aside for the duplicates of Steeleye. There was only the merest chance that any of them would be killed, a chance worth taking.

And it had worked. Or almost. For Steeleye was just in time to see Yellow reel back from a thin line that zipped into the chamber. The line expanded as Steeleye looked through the high window of the castle and a blaster fired a deadly shot across the whole of the upper half of the Pierrot's graceful body, splattering him over the monitors with which he had sought to kill Steeleye. That was the finish of Yellow. Caught off balance for the first time in 7,000 years he had not been prepared for any attack, least of all the vicious, unmerciful agggression of the Sideways Man. And Kimber knew that if he disposed of Yellow he would be disposing of the solutions to all the clues but one of the crossword planned to rid him of his power. The line had returned and Kimber had vanished into the Wideways.

Chapter 12

It was like the end of a great tournament, or a practical joke gone wrong, ending in disaster. The castle felt empty, and with the departure of the two aggressors the tension suddenly dropped to nothing and the vargs came out of their hiding places to wander aimlessly through the decimated corridors and down into the hallway where they all assembled.

The battle was over but not the war. A sense of uselessness spread over the unwelcome occupants of the castle on the Crystal Planet as Chaos joined them from Tristor. Yellow's remains were witness to a deed which had badly backfired. Steeleye felt guilt at the needless slaughter. He had never intended it but was the direct cause of it.

"Well, that was a right cock-up, wasn't it?" Vandal tried to put a lighter note to the events, but it fell on dulled ears. The vargs sat about on the wide stair base, each with his cloak wrapped round close against the cold.

Steeleye and Chaos stood before them at the base of the stair and for a few moments no one spoke.

"There was an old man who looked like a clown,
They say his name was Yellow.
His hair was full golden, his face tanned a brown,
In fact, quite a good-looking fellow.
For thousands of years a castle he squired,
With ambitions to gather great power,
But then came the day when things quite backfired,
And plans, well laid once turned right sour.
He died in dimensions he quite understood,
While trying to get to another.
And amongst all the carnage, drowned well in his blood.
The secret desired he did smother.
But one in the gathering, mighty and strong,
A man made of Steel so they say,

Was set to put right a most terrible wrong.
And so it was written on Life-making day.
For Steeleye and Kimber commenced their great fight,
The day that Yellow died,
To pitch against each the sum of their might
In future brave tales to abide."

The sound of Vandal's voice echoed through the huge cold chamber and a feeling of destiny sank heavily on the shoulders of Steeleye.

As they stood, not knowing what they should do to set the next moves in motion, two huge figures appeared at the doorway, two very familiar figures, both four metres tall, and both, while obviously immensely powerful, also strangely calm and wise.

"We thought it might be advantageous to Zrost to undertake a little research into a number of the contrivances in this castle."

Tousle's familiar measured tone sent shivers of pleasure through Steeleye and Chaos as they turned to face the Android's steady progress toward the gathering.

"You are most welcome both, Tousle and Hamgar, perhaps I could introduce you to my friends, the vargs. They have all aided me in a task which seems to have ended sadly. Meet our resident poet and lyricist, Vandal."

"Ah, at last, the creator of Men, lo he cometh, solemn and mighty."

"Shut up, Vandal, you soft-headed vagrant." Chaos smacked Vandal on the back and sent him reeling across the floor.

"I am pleased that we meet, Vandal, my colleague Timor has told me much of your exploits with him. I am sorry we could not talk when you visited Zrost but I was much occupied in a task of some significance."

"I imagine that Kimber will return here before time has passed too long, so that we should move with haste." Hamgar spoke.

"Yes, in fact he could return through any time and be here before now should he wish." Steeleye feared Kimber's games.

"We can't shut the door against its lord, he's like a rat and can squirm under any entrance."

"Come then, let's see what there is for the Eumigs here."

Vandal walked with Tousle, fascinated by his colossal size.

"What will you do, Tousle, take the stuff with you?"

"No, we shall look into things and make records on our tapes. We don't need the goods when we can make them ourselves. All we need is the way to make them. Shall we start in the museum? I'm sure Boy would welcome an opportunity to investigate further the machinery Yellow showed him so briefly."

"You bet." Boy bounced up beside the two, making a strangely comic line-up of figures, Tousle towering over Vandal by nearly two metres and Vandal over Boy by nearly one.

They all three passed into the Cantelevator, followed by Steeleye and Chaos. The rest of the vargs took up posts of watch throughout the castle.

Tousle lifted the cover off the first device in the museum. It was tall, sitting square on a podium and rising two metres from it. It slightly sloped away, like a desk with a roller cover and on the front were hand controls. Tousle had recorded translator tapes into his memory so that he could understand the Kimbernium inscriptions, but this one was different. The language made no sense to anyone.

"Come, Hamgar, a code for you to crack. This language has its origins in the eighth galaxy I would say."

"Not at all, Tousle, more in the region of fourth millenia Tarvos. That's for sure."

"Oh come now, look at those character slopes, the Tarvos languages of the fourth were squarer, don't you think?"

Tousle and Hamgar began a long dissertation circling round and round their different versions of what they believed the language to be. They had disagreed, one way or another for as long as anyone could recall. This occasion was no exception. As the argument continued Boy piped up from near to something much smaller, unveiled next to the first.

"Hey you two, cut out the noise and come and see what I've found. It's got Univerlinguous on it."

The two Eumigs moved to behind Boy and peered over him at the device. "A translator. Perfect, now we shall see who is right."

Hamgar grasped the hand machine shaped like a torch with a thin beam escape at one end and a viewer at the other. On the top was an audio outlet, and the word "Translator" printed in ten different tongues.

Hamgar beamed one end onto one of the words on the large instrument.

"This language is known as Calvanese and the words shown are translated into Univerlinguous as follows: 'Random selector'." Hamgar moved the translator on to another phrase and the machine spoke again: "Three slot lose or gain." Then on further: "Unbias decision selection." And on again: "Prize award." And lastly: "Credit."

"What on Zrost is it?"

"It isn't on Zrost, Hamgar, but it's perfectly obvious what it is."

"All right, clever Richard, tell us what it is."

"Well, it says what it is, doesn't it? It's a random decision selector, like tossing a coin only you can have more than two alternatives, you can have as many as you want. All you do is feed in the alternatives and hey presto you get a selection. Probably works on some sort of infinite matrix drop, giving the perfect random."

"What about the ones marked 'Three slot lose or gain', and 'Prize award' and 'Credit', and what have they to do with unbiased decisions?"

"Hm, how should I know . . .?"

"It's a one-armed bandit," Boy chirped, looking at another machine.

"A what?"

"A one-armed bandit, it's obvious. You put a credit notation in here and you press the 'Three slot lose or gain' button. In the old days you pulled an arm and the three characters rolled round. If they stopped in the right combination you won a hundred times your gamble or whatever. Obvious."

He continued to gaze at another device then moved casually, his hands behind his back, to the gambling machine.

"He's right you know."

"I do believe he is."

"Well, aren't you going to have a go?" Boy offered.

"Have a go at what?"

"Putting a credit in, and gambling, of course. Dad? Give me a credit please, I'd like to win my first fortune." Steeleye handed boy a credit notation. Boy adjusted it to Univercredit accounts and slipped it into the slot. Several lights came on and turned off again then a central screen lit up and three small designs showed. They began turning at different speeds. The whirring of their movement rose to a peak and then slowed to nothing. The machine coughed and let out a kind of hiss followed by a brief answer.

"No correlation." And that was that.

Boy tried again and the others moved onto other devices leaving him absorbed in his gambling spree.

As they went Steeleye turned to Tousle and asked him:

"What is Calvanese?"

"Wait, I will search my records." Tousle remained silent as his brain responded to the question.

"Calvanese is spoken by the Calves who lived 'Zrost termination' from C-1349th to +64th and died through cloning overburden and clone wars. The planet remains intact in the fifth 'Wander' section of galaxy 8763453/4657 but there is some evidence that a black hole, fifty light years distant is growing sufficiently to take in the planet. No Eumig has visited, it is beyond the reaches of our requirements and our spatial research plans at present. We are expecting to cover that sector in thirteen hundred years Zrost termination from now. That is the sum of our records." Tousle remained quiet.

"So what connection would there be between Calve and here, or Calve and Kimber?"

"There is no record of such a connection in my records."

"Hm." Steeleye remained thoughtful as he looked at the next exhibit. Every so often the one-armed bandit sang out its chime of "no correlation", and Steeleye's mind, somewhere in the back rooms clocked up the credits.

Tousle and Hamgar were at it again with the next article.

"This is an automatic substance analyser. Simple, we've made a better one on Zrost."

"No Hamgar, it is no such thing. It's a sophisticated drink dispenser used in entertainment halls or in private apartments, obsolete now of course with the recent Eumig innovations into molecular storage units."

Chaos pulled one of the levers on the machine and it began to play a sort of music.

"It sings too," she jibed at them.

"A sound synthesiser, Hamgar, a sound synthesiser, obviously."

It made the most extrordinary vibrations in every tone level imaginable. It changed its music from one form to another, sounding like the old moog synthesisers.

"Quite a machine that."

"Got it." There was a terrific belch from the machine that Boy had been hassling now for a full ten minutes. The sound was reminiscent of an oversized gourmet after a midnight feast of ale and radishes.

"Random selection correlates, prize."

"I get a prize, Steeleye. I get a prize!" Boy leapt in the air with excitement, waiting for his prize. But for a moment nothing happened. "Whassamader with it, where's my prize?"

The machine coughed and spluttered, evidently not accustomed to handing out prizes.

"It probably hasn't had to do this in a million years," Tousle suggested.

"It hasn't been around that long," added Hamgar.

"How do you know? It could have been through half a dozen time systems and landed up here like a floating bottle."

"A what?" Hamgar became confused whenever Tousle began to proselytise at him, especially when he used terms Hamgar had never heard of.

"You spend too much time in that 'book' library." Hamgar's only remaining tack.

"Hey, look, there's something coming out of the thing, look."

Boy leapt about in front of the bandit as it regurgitated a long, bent piece of hard material, shaped like an obtuse-angled letter L of the old Earth English language.

"What is it, Dad?"

"I don't know, Boy, let me see."

He held out the strange slender curved prize. It measured a metre in length, even though it was bent in the middle and its flat sharp edges were smoothly tempered to look like a pair of full wings without a body.

"It's a boomerang," said Tousle. They all gathered around Boy's prize.

"What is a boomerang?"

"That is."

"No no, what does a boomerang do?"

"It flies, come I'll show you. It has some rather amusing, but do not be fooled, also extremely dangerous properties. Perhaps we should recommune outside the castle and I will give you a demonstration."

And so they all went out and stood a hundred metres from the castle door.

"Now, if I am correct, which is likely, you hold the device at one end and you hurl it hard away from the body, like a Sylvan fighter's knife. The only difference being that this will turn in the air because of its aerodynamic qualities and return to us. It is advisable to keep the eyes upon its flight path in case it should hit one in the back of the neck while one is not looking. A boomerang of this size could easily decapitate a human head from its body. So, watch where it goes and prepare to duck. I will try to assess its potential trajectory mathematically and throw it correctly but without knowing the prevailing wind conditions I cannot be entirely accurate."

Tousle flung the boomerang hard. In fact he threw it in that heavy gravity atmosphere so that it travelled nearly two hundred and fifty metres before it began to return. He had only used a little muscle behind it, in case it went into orbit! You think I'm joking? Well, you haven't seen Tousle.

Eventually the boomerang returned and landed neatly and squarely at Boy's feet.

"Clever dick," commented Hamgar. "Lucky fluke."

"I assure you that it was not. I knew exactly where it would land."

"Wow, let me have a go."

Boy threw the boomerang and it flew high in the air, turned and rocketed back at them all with more speed than it had departed.

As it came closer Steeleye could see that it was going to hit Vandal. He put one huge powerful arm out and grasped it as it slipped through the air just above Vandal's head.

"Chee, my head was due for a hole . . . I think."

"No question, at that speed and with the probably thin skull it would have driven at least ten centimetres into your brain before stopping, even allowing for kinetics." Tousle was showing off.

"What's all this about a thin skull? Everyone else calls me thick head."

"A powerful weapon, Boy. You had better practice well with it. Keep close to the castle door though. We cannot afford to let Kimber see you out here alone. Storm, would you take personal watch over him?"

"My pleasure, Steeleye, we will compete with the er . . . boomerang."

"Good. Come, let's return to the museum, there are still some treasures more to examine."

Chapter 13

In the days when battles were fought in the jungles, when you chased your foe through thickets with a knife and a stick, he would set traps for you. He would tie a sprung sapling down to a stake and attach it to a loop of rope so that when you stepped into the rope the sapling would be released and you would end upside-down, conveniently placed to have your throat slit. Such were the dangers of jungle warfare. Kimber knew that Steeleye would be after him in the Wideways and his instincts were the same.

Because the complexities of time are so much greater than those of three dimensional space and matter, there was extensive opportunity for preparing death traps. And when you are in the jungle of the Wideways you need to be aware of every atom about you. Kimber set up the most devious series of 'blunder-wonders' you could ever hope to find in a practical joke kit. His dexterity in sideswipes and flour bags, to say nothing of the rope tricks and stink bombs would make your mouth hang open, while he popped a lizard in. But Kimber was not joking, his intentions were to lead Steeleye and his band into some very nasty holes through the ways that he knew well, the Wideways.

And he announced his intentions through the next instrument which took their fancy. Steeleye, Chaos, Tousle, Hamgar and Vandal, all settled around a huge featureless contraption relieved of its great transparent cover and standing naked, waiting for discovery. There was little to aid the researchers for on the surface of the device there were no words, no buttons nor other controls. It was flat, perfectly featureless and offering no clues.

"Well, don't tell me neither of you have any idea what it is."

Vandal nudged Tousle's side, thinking his arm would sink into a rib cage had Tousle had one, but he bruised his arm severely on the reinforced skin. Not only that but Tousle ignored him, more intent on extracting some diagnosis from the thing before him.

"Coaw, when did you last have a milk bath?" Vandal rubbed his elbow.

"Milk bath?" Tousle turned to him, always fascinated by irrelevancies.

"Goat's milk, cow's milk, Tar's milk, take your choice, they all soften the skin and make you delicate." He spoke the last few words with a touch to his face, feigning affectation.

"Foolishness." Well, what would you expect Tousle to say?

"I think it's a preserver," Hamgar suggested, not thinking anything of the kind.

"A preserver of what?"

"Of anything that needs preserving," said with some determination, but not much.

"I see, then would you care to open it and put something that needs preserving inside, so that we may observe your hypothesis."

Before Hamgar could reply the contraption changed colour before them. It turned a dull red shade and then altered again, becoming opaque then clearer until soon it was almost transparent.

"Ooh-er," observed Vandal.

The device shone from within and a thin straight line appeared.

"Oh dear." Another Vandal offering. The whole company backed off including Steeleye, whose eye glowed slightly in anticipation. The Sideways Man appeared.

"Good, I am glad you are here, for I have something important to tell you. Something that concerns one of your number, Steeleye. It would seem that you would wish to disturb the balance of my power over the Wideways. I imagine that you have dug up some prophesy which designates your right to take my power from me. So sad that you still believe in predestination. It is nonsense, I can change any future in any way I like, yours too. However, in the light of your determination it will be easier for me to demonstrate my powers to you in the open. I have set a place and time for an encounter between myself and Steeleye. If you would be kind enough to reconvene on the planet Earth in the year 130,000,000 B.C., during the period known as the Cretaceous. I am prone to dramatic gestures, and I rather fancy having a look at a dinosaur. Please be my guest and use the time chamber. I will expect you on the first full moon of that year on the plateau instructed into the teleport time machine." The device became opaque once more and the Sideways Man was gone.

"Rather you than me," Vandal muttered, turning from the screen.

"Me too," said Boy.

"Back to Earth again, and so far back. It will take a while to get there I imagine, but then we have all the time in the world."

"Do we?" asked Vandal, forever chirping his questions.

"Of course, it matters not when we depart, we shall arrive there at the appointed time. In fact we are there now." Tousle turned from Vandal to Steeleye.

"Eh?" responded the young varg, but no one was going to explain. "Come, Steeleye, there is much to prepare."

"We are going back to an age known on Earth as the Mesozoic or middle life period of the planet's history. It lasted about 160,000,000 years and ranged through the Triassic, the Jurassic and the Cretaceous periods.

"What happened before then?" Boy asked Tousle as they sat comfortably in the long-distance machine.

"Before then was the Palaeozoic periods or ancient life and the Proterozoic, some 600,000,000 Earth years before civilised man."

"When did Earth start?" Boy sat, fascinated by Tousle's knowledge.

"The Eumigs have pitched it at 4,859 million years before man emerged."

"Wow, if we get out of this alive can we go back there and watch?"

"There's nothing to see, it's all fire and brimstone, much more exciting to go 5,000 million years into man's future, you might see something interesting then."

"Like what?" Boy chirped.

"The end of the sun, a new race, very exciting."

They remained silent for a while as the huge machine rushed back into the past. The date was flashing up on the wall and as they sat waiting it moved into Earth time dates. The dates they saw were moving through the 2800s when man was soon to leave for Zrost.

"The dawn of the Eumigs." Tousle spoke quietly as the figures rolled backwards almost too fast to see now.

"Can't we stop and watch for a while?" Boy asked.

"On the way back, Boy, on the way back." Steeleye spoke to his son, his voice tinged with unexpected tension. Chaos moved closer to him and rested her head against his shoulder.

Time travel was sadly an uneventful experience for there were no jolts or jumps, no changes in feeling or awareness. In this rapid, technically advanced machine there was no contact with the fleeting worlds they passed.

Soon they were entering the ancient periods of Earth and skimming back through millions of years until it began to slow.

The instructions of the machine were precise, to set its cargo down at the predetermined plateau on the young planet.

The machine hovered in the time alley and phased back its walls revealing the landing place. It was in their hands now to make a way down onto the surface and the time chamber would remain for their return.

The ground below was not quite as they had expected. It was oppresive; swamps and huge river deltas that spread like vast seas across the land. There were patches of lush vegetation, intersected with rank marshland. Here and there could be seen the huge reptiles, heads bent as they grazed peacefully.

"Wow, what a dump," muttered Vandal distastefully. "Not much a varg could do here."

"I believe we are somewhere in North America, or what will emerge as North America," Tousle observed.

"What about the dinosaurs?"

"They're huge, I never thought they'd be so big," Boy said.

"We can put up a force barrier for an arena, that should keep them out." Tousle pressed a control and they set gently down onto the surface. He took out a machine from his belt and touched a contact. Nothing happened.

"Kimber has spiked my field control."

"To be expected." Steeleye paced the soft earth.

There were towering mountain ranges across one side of the land mass, untamed by weather and water erosion. Where they stood was flat, and comprised the largest single piece of uninterrupted land in sight. It was surrounded by water and swamp.

As they stood a colossal creature loomed into sight and trudged towards them, stopping about thirty metres distant.

"Look, what's that?"

"It's an Iguanodon, herbivorous, doesn't like meat. It might have a go at us but I doubt it. Look, it's not very certain."

The creature turned its head to one side as though trying to puzzle out what it should do next. Then it blundered off in another direction.

"We had better make preparations. I think most of us should set up a ring round Steeleye to protect him against these creatures, we don't want too many interruptions. Who has weapons?"

Various devices were produced.

"Try them, Vandal, blast that tree over there." Vandal did so and the tree disintegrated.

"Good, so he hasn't put us out of action. Form a wide ring, about forty metres, Vandal you take Boy with you. Anything that looks like it's going to attack or become a nuisance, just blow its head off, no wounding, we can't afford second chances."

"I'm going up this tree." Boy scamperer off with Vandal close behind brandishing the blaster.

"I doubt your weapons will be a lot of use against Kimber so don't try," Tousle shouted after them.

"Go now, Tousle, look after Chaos, I shall want to see you all intact after this is over." Chaos stood on tiptoe and kissed Steeleye, then left with Tousle.

Steeleye stood alone now in the midst of a land he knew nothing of and would never have chosen to visit. Nevertheless it was a land which would be the home of his kind one day. They had all expected Kimber to arrive, stand before Steeleye and fight but they were quite wrong, for Kimber was not one to give advantages and he knew Steeleye's strength too well. Far away, in the sky the line quivered and sped to earth without expanding. Steeleye saw him coming but chose to ignore it, and turned away, walking over to a small shrub that grew nearby. He sent out strong TI messages at Kimber, bombarding him with aggression and threat and then changed his tack, transmitting thought waves to jibe and humiliate him. As he walked he formed a plan. Then he turned to see that the Sideways Man still descending but in an arc positioned to end in front of Steeleye. Steeleye turned back again, and began to burn the ground, backing away as he did so. His eye scorched a wide area of the earth leaving it black and scarred. The angle was wide and anyone landing on the ground at that point would be burnt to a cinder. He turned and did the same on his other side so that soon he was standing at the centre of a smoking and charred piece of ground. There was nowhere for Kimber to stand within twenty metres of Steeleye who stood near the still green shrub and waited.

"I find your welcome disappointing, Steeleye. I had thought that you might act the part of the gentleman and shake my hand before we began."

Steeleye did not answer.

"You are like the man who paints his floor the wrong way, backing himself into a corner from which he cannot retreat. Foolish, Steeleye, very foolish." Kimber raised a blaster and levelled it at Steeleye.

One quick flash from the eye jolted it from Kimber's hand to land on the smouldering ground. Kimber cursed.

"Some eye you have there." He produced another weapon but this time turned it upon Boy in the tree.

"Try again, Steeleye. One glint of heat and I will dispose of your stupid child." As he levelled the blaster he looked at Steeleye.

"What do you want? I thought the fight was between you and me."

"So it was, and so it shall be if you will permit me to land."

Steeleye knew that his skills were as great in flight as they were on solid ground so he pushed into the air himself to come level with Kimber but with ten metres separating them.

"Better still, Kimber, I will rise to your level. The earth will take a while to cool and we have no refreshments to offer you just now."

"You play games with me, Steeleye, I assure you it will not be to your advantage to mock."

The Sideways Man suddenly turned from Steeleye, slipping into the Wideways and becoming that ubiquitous line again. The line lengthened until it was twice Steeleye's height and at its top was a sharp point. It lifted into the air as though a giant athlete were carrying it ready to throw and as it drew back it pointed its head at Steeleye's body.

With the swiftness of a javelin it was cast forward. Steeleye reacted only just quickly enough. As it hurtled towards him he shifted his position above it and it swept past only to turn immediately and rush back again like a computerised missile. It came again even faster than before and as it moved Kimber's voice spoke from the air above them.

"You are a man, Steeleye, so I will accord you the privilege of dying like a man."

Steeleye dodged again and blasted the spear with his eye at full power. The line crippled but recovered rapidly, as though the blast had dislodged Kimber slightly but not enough to hurt him.

"Come mighty Eumig eye, surely you can do better than that."

Steeleye levelled a longer blast at the spear as it rushed

again, swerving through the air, trying to avoid the intense heat. But Steeleye's aim was true and the heat he generated prevented Kimber from rushing at him. The line vanished for a second and then reappeared behind Steeleye. This time it was equipped with another weapon, a long smooth blaster attached like a gun to a fighter plane. The blaster fired as the spear moved towards Steeleye's body and caught his tunic, burning the sleeve from his arm.

Steeleye swept high into the air, travelling two hundred metres in a few seconds. The spear turned and the blaster fired again but made no impression on its target as Steeleye had simultaneously spread a wide angle of fire from his Eumig eye, which cushioned the atomic blast and dispersed it into nothingness.

The Sideways Man metamorphosed yet again – this time into a ball, which started to spin, rotating so fast that it was no more than a blur. Only by the turbulence of the air could Steeleye detect its movement towards him.

He gave it a wide berth, flying across the air in a long trajectory. The circle turned with him. Steeleye dodged but not fast enough and the smouldering Kimber hit him so violently on the side, sending his body spinning, that he hit the ground with a crash before he realised what was happening. The Sideways Man wasted no time, turned into the spear again and plummeted towards the ground.

The distance he had to travel was some seventy-five metres to Steeleye's body and exactly at the instant Steeleye landed Tousle saw a reptile thundering towards them through the undergrowth. He calculated rapidly that in a few seconds the Megalosaurus would collide with Steeleye's body if it was permitted free run.

"Leave the animal, let it through." By TI transmission he communicated to the others nearby and the great carnivore lumbered by, heading straight for Steeleye prone on the ground. But also for the flying Kimber spear.

At precisely the right moment Tousle shot a tractor beam from his shoulder at Steeleye's body and carried it three metres out of the track of the monster. It was timed to coincide with the creature's arrival between Kimber and

Steeleye and though it had no effect on the slow reactions of the animal it effectively removed Kimber's target. The spear instead sank deep into the Megalosaurus's shoulder. It bucked into the air and shook itself violently. The contortions of this powerfully muscular giant were jarring the spear deeper into its shoulder. Steeleye looked up to see the great six metre dinosaur racking itself with the spear jammed soundly into its body. Kimber must have been stunned by the blow for it was seconds before he began to attempt to extricate himself.

Steeleye did not help him. He was concussed and badly bruised himself and he reasoned that the animal would give Kimber a nasty time before it finally shook him loose. The speared line suddenly began to glow red and burned a hole in the shoulder area of the blundering animal. The heat was so intense that once Kimber was free and standing beside the Megalosaurus the hole in its body covered nearly a metre in diameter and it lay like a small hill, dead.

Kimber leapt up onto its side, standing over Steeleye, he was about to deliver a fatal shot to his still dizzy victim when a long, bent heavy object hit him square on the side of his head. It rebounded to the ground leaving Kimber unable to stand straight. He fell off the body of the animal and landed on Steeleye, rolling off clutching his head. Then he quivered into his fine line and disappeared.

Boy's boomerang had been well aimed.

Steeleye stood up and Tousle summoned the time machine. They all stood together and the machine took them back to the castle without delay.

"Tough ain't he?" said Vandal. "You're going to have a rough ride chasing that one across the Wideways."

"It must be done though, I will not let him go now."

The journey seemed to last forever but they finally arrived at the time chamber, and Steeleye, followed closely by Tousle and Vandal rushed into the Wideways chamber.

"Where to?"

"Calve." Steeleye spoke surely. And the journey began.

Chapter 14

"Oh boy, if this is Calve, I'm a Hebridian heifer."

They had stopped somehow, somewhere unexpected.

"Where do you get these expressions, Vandal?" They walked down a dusty, windblown ghost town, tumbledown shacks and doorless shanties lined an empty street littered with tumbleweed.

"I read book tapes, and I read about this place somewhere, I thought we just left Earth, we're back again a few hundred million years on."

"It does look a little that way." Tousle could get no bearing, no point of reference. The planet looked normal from every angle, but it could not be Calve for the time was wrong. It was either Earth twentieth century or an identical planet in another location with all the characteristics of that planet and that time.

"Look, someone must live here, there's washing hanging out on that piece of rope over there, covered in sand and dust but it's wet."

"Wet? In this climate, how do you know it's wet?"

"Look, it's sagging, dripping in fact. Unless somebody just sprayed it with a hose pipe it was recently hung out. It hasn't rained here in ten years."

The street was dry and the buildings on either side were wooden. They stopped together at the sound of voices to their right, from a small bar just off the street.

"Shall we go in?"

"I'd better remain here, they might panic at the sight of me," Tousle advised.

"Oh come on now, you're not that ugly," Vandal jibed.

"I was not referring to . . ."

"Only joking, only joking, come on, Steeleye, let's see if they've got some of that scoshwhisky in there."

Steeleye and Vandal walked into the bar. The occupants

turned for a moment and looked at them. Their eyes followed the massive form of Steeleye and then looked down at the small varg.

The cursory glance from the lads around the bar and at the tables was soon over and they turned again to their several interests.

"Got any whisky, brother?"

The barman looked vaguely in Vandal's direction but ignored him completely.

They sat at an empty table and watched developments.

The voices of two of the men in the bar suddenly grew louder. One man stood up and drew a revolver from his belt, he aimed the weapon at the chest of the other and fired. A huge blast of flame shot from the gun and a bullet lodged in the chest of the other man, blood rushing from the wound inflicted directly over the heart. The man jumped, his body kicked by the force of the shot but he did not fall, continuing to remonstrate at the other man who fired another shot, this time straight into the fellow's head, blasting a hideous hole through one eye and blowing half his brains out at the back. The man should long have been dead but he still cursed and swore, wiping the blood from his face with one careless hand. He drew his own gun and fired two deadly shots into the other man's face. Steeleye and Vandal winced as the man with his back to them lost at least half of his brain tissue. But the man remained standing for a moment and then sat down and they continued in a quieter fashion. No one paid the slightest attention to them.

"I see," said Vandal in a sort of bemused, disbelieving tone.

As they watched the two fighting men the wounds on their heads and bodies healed, the flesh creeping over and leaving only a shadowed indentation. Within five or six minutes there was no evidence that they had fought at all.

"Have you noticed something?" asked Steeleye.

"Ho, ho, you're joking of course."

"No, I mean, apart from the instant healing, something else?"

"What?"

"They're getting older."

"Are they?"

"All of them, getting older by the minute. Watch those two over there, the ones facing us. Watch, there are lines growing on their faces, every second they're ageing."

"Cubin christ, you're right. Look that one over there's going to peg out any minute, right in his seat, look, he's going, going—" there was a thump and the old fellow, younger only minutes before, heaved over from his chair and slumped to the floor—"gone."

"And another, behind you, two more, three." As Steeleye spoke three men, the one who had just had his brains blown out and survived the experience, keeled over and died.

Steeleye looked back at the first one to die and his body was already starting to disintegrate. Within three minutes there was nothing but a heap of dust which blew away as the door of the saloon opened.

"Cor blimey, you could knock me down with a blow to the head, look, replacements."

Sure enough four men walked in, young men, and took the vacated seats about the bar room. And as Steeleye and Vandal watched the other men in the room fell like flies from their chairs, crashing to the ground and disintegrating almost as fast as a blasted warrior. Each time one went down a replacement would enter and take his place. Everyone talked and laughed, shot each other regularly and generally drank a lot of some potent brew or other.

"Do you think it's the stuff they're drinking?" queried Vandal.

Steeleye smiled vaguely.

"I mean, it's strong stuff, maybe we should try and persuade them onto fruit juices or something."

"No, no, it's a time factor, this place's wrong, there's some time change going on, we're in a different dimension."

"Let's have a look around a bit more, this is getting depressing."

They left the bar and joined Tousle who had noticed the effect.

"Funny lot in there," Vandal remarked to Tousle as they set off down the deserted street.

"Yes, had a few out here too, dropping every few seconds, didn't seem to notice me."

"Surprise, you're not the easiest person to miss. They seemed to see *us* in there didn't they, Steeleye?"

"I'm not sure they saw us, they might have seen the doors open and some kind of image. You went to the bar and got no response so we might just had been blurs to them."

"Don't look now but there's a guy up on a hotel balcony and I think he's got a rifle aimed at us." Vandal spoke out of the corner of his mouth and Steeleye turned, his eye glowing red.

"Stay where y'ar, don't move, I wanna speak to you."

The fellow leapt down from the balcony at least ten metres from the ground and landed with a resounding crunch. His body crumpled and cracked and every bone in his legs and pelvis must have been shattered. He remained on the ground observing his legs for a moment as they shifted about inside his trousers in the most comical fashion.

"Look, his legs is doin' a dance, mendin' themselves, ain't they?" Vandal started to roll his eyes, feigning madness.

The cowboy stood up again, the mending process evidently complete.

"Howdy. You strangers?"

"Well, we're certainly not familiar, we don't live too nearby," Vandal parried.

"Don't joke with me, boy, you've come from another planet ain't yer?"

"What's the name of this place?" asked Tousle, observing the strangely ageing cowboy.

"Earth, what do you think?"

"And the country?"

"Country, there ain't no country here, this is just Earth."

"What year?"

"1946."

"How come you know so much about aliens, have there been a lot?"

"Oh yeh, we get them through here all the time, every hour."

The cowboy's face was gradually ageing like the others and his back began to bend.

"You don't get any older, do yer? Can't you stand still a bit – stop moving so fast," he commented at the three standing before him; as he crumpled slowly to the ground and died.

"He never did get it out." Vandal looked at the disappearing dust.

"No, they don't get a lot of time, do they?"

They walked a little further, Tousle all the time quiet.

"I've been searching," he said at last.

"Searching what?" asked Vandal.

"My memory banks, something he said about the date, 1946."

"Yes?"

"Well, something in our records mentions a possible disaster on an Earth in 1946. There was a meteorite, a very large one, headed for an Earth."

"What do you mean, *an* Earth?"

"Well, Earth in one of its dimensions. The Earth that we knew before the Wideways. This meteorite only missed Earth by a very small margin, a few million kilometres or some such, I was just wondering whether this could be the Earth it hit."

"But you just said it missed." Vandal was dumb.

"You're dumb, Vandal, we're in the Wideways remember? Every single event in time has an infinite number of alternatives, so if the meteorite missed Earth in one dimension it was bound to have hit it in another, maybe this one."

"But the chances must be almost infinite." Steeleye looked up at the sky, lengthening his telescopic sight to its maximum.

"Yes, the chances are pretty remote but we're forgetting Kimber."

"You mean he might have buggered the works in the Wideways machine?"

"Look." Steeleye pointed. Tousle lengthened the lenses in both eyes and focussed on the meteorite.

"Let's get out of here."

"How for Cubin's sake, how?"

"Back into the Wideways, idiot, turn, think TI back into the Wideways, and get at least fifty dimensions away, this thing will hit on that many dimensions." They turned and vanished, only within seconds of the total annihilation of Earth 3,345,764 in the Wideways line-up.

"This is like bloody Dr. Who."

"Dr. Who?" asked Tousle.

"Yes."

"What?"

"We keep on coming out at funny places. Where are we now?"

"Who's Dr. Who?" Tousle persisted.

"What?"

"Who?"

"Who do you mean what? I mean what do you mean who?" Vandal enjoyed these games immensely.

"Dr. Who?"

"What Dr. Who, what?"

"Now listen, you horrible little vagrant, you said something about a Dr. Who, I want to know who Who is?"

"Who's who, a list of well-known people."

"What?"

"What's what, a list of . . . "

Tousle brought a huge fist lightly down upon Vandal's head and the young varg crumpled to the ground.

"Please keep your sledgehammers to yourself."

They stood on an open plain, completely devoid of anything but one small hut. It stood fifty metres from them and was built from wood, about ten metres square and as many tall, it stood amidst rolling vegetation, sloping hills and valleys in a land evidently fertile enough to support life.

But there was no sign of any cities or towns. Tousle lifted high into the air.

"Nothing, no sign of any other life, no structures, nothing." But this little hut.

There was a river flowing gently past the hut and propped up on the bank was a fishing rod, its twine trailing across the gentle murmuring water. Seated in a deckchair behind it, as they moved round to a different view, was a long-legged man, dressed in a chequered shirt and jeans, a battered canvas hat on his head. He looked content, as though he had actually got away from it all at last.

As they approached, he spoke to them without turning.

"'Day, gentlemen, please join me, I might catch you a fresh salmon if you wait a while. I imagine you could do with something to eat. You must have travelled far."

"We would be delighted, deeelighted." Vandal sat down next to the fellow on the river bank and settled immediately into this unknown environment in truly vagrant fashion.

Tousle X-rayed the walls of the hut and saw nothing inside but a bunk bed, a few cooking facilities, an old stove and some clothes hung on the walls. No weapons, no travel equipment.

"Live here alone, do you?" asked Vandal after a long pause, in which the man lit a pipe and began puffing contentedly.

"Yes, just me."

"No one else anywhere on the whole planet?"

"No one, I made sure before I came."

"Ah." Vandal felt that he shouldn't intrude too far into this man's privacy. Tousle, however, did not suffer from the same hang-ups, he was simply aware of the potential danger.

"Have you been here for long?"

"Are you detectives?"

"No, just travellers."

"Me too." The response more or less said "mind your own business."

"Ever heard of a planet named Calve?" Steeleye asked.

"Nope." No indication.

They stood, all three of them, on one side of the seated man and after the nil response from him Vandal got up and walked round the other side. He jumped and then stifled his reaction. Trying to prevent the man from seeing what he did Vandal began an elaborate mime routine, directed at Steeleye and Tousle, attempting to indicate to them that they should come over his side and have a look at what he had found. He definitely did not wish the man to know of his discovery.

The sight of Tousle wandering about, his hands behind his back like an innocent schoolboy was very funny. Any minute he would start to whistle, just to complete the picture. When he reached the other side he took in the mystery and then sat down on the ground, setting his brain to work to find out how the man could be a man on one side and something else very different on the other. As he did so the seated fellow stood up and faced Steeleye. He stepped closer and Steeleye could see his two-sided face very clearly. One side was that of a man, a very good-looking man of middle age. The other side was hideous, rough and pitted, with the eye gone and the ear larger. There was no hair on his head or face. The whole of that side of the body was naked and had been severely burned, scarred. The arm was limp and the leg shrivelled to the bone, though the muscles were just able to hold his body up.

Steeleye backed off instinctively as the extraordinary effigy before him fingered a button on his belt. He sweated heavily, the moisture pouring down his face and over his naked side. His eye was popping out of its socket and Tousle suddenly, without any warning rushed across the space between them and carried the awful creature in his arms, lifted him above his body and was about to hurl him through the air when he exploded. A massive blast and the entire body of the schizoid man erupted, his head flying off in one direction, great hunks of flesh thrown across the air. There was nothing left whole but the head. Tousle turned to them both, holding his arms before them. Both his hands had gone and much of his chest cavity had been blasted away.

"It seems that I shall have to leave you temporarily to facilitate repair. Remember that everything from now on might be booby-trapped. Do not approach anything except with caution. I will return as soon as I have some new hands." With that, Tousle turned sideways and disappeared.

"Gordon Bennett."

"Stay on your father planet, Steeleye, you are not needed elsewhere. Keep away from Calve, it will destroy you."

The voice issued from the head of the exploded body. Even the mouth moved.

"So much for Kimber's games!" Steeleye was angry.

"Hey, me Tarzan." Vandal's words were not really meant to mock. The sight of Steeleye rising up from the fullness of his height to an even greater height was thoroughly awe-inspiring.

"How do you do that?"

Steeleye had learnt the old tricks of the Sylvans well, and now he was going to use a few of them on Kimber.

"You will see some strange shapes, Vandal, do not be alarmed for the Sylvans taught me the ways of molecular re-structuring, now I shall show Kimber a few tricks of my own."

"Don't go too fast, I'll never keep up with you."

"I'll tie you to me."

"Yerch . . ."' Vandal was swept from his feet as the huge giant moved off into the Wideways at astonishing speed.

Chapter 15

"What the Cubin devil is that?"

"A black hole, an implosion of a dying star. Somewhere in there is the Kimber hideaway."

"How do you know for sure?"

"The Wideways tell. You can't travel through them without leaving some TI transmission and Kimber's TI leads here. This place used to be owned by some Lord of Calve, and Kimber took it over. But he will try to lead us away from it if he knows we are here."

"That's why we came such a roundabout route in this old crate?"

Steeleye had stolen a rather ancient space launch from Calve in its older days, taken it through a time field to arrive within sight of the black hole.

"Yes, with any luck he won't be expecting us."

"Sure, but how the devil do we get across the distance in an old junk heap like this? We'll never make it. Must be at least fifty light years."

"We can't go any nearer anyway, we'd get sucked in. It's only because we're so small that we haven't already."

"So? What's the plan, master?"

"We're going to do a little time-tinkering first, give Kimber a nasty shock."

"Goody goody."

Steeleye slipped out of the launch, surrounded in a force field circulating air inside it. He put a field round the launch, tight-fitting and strong and then slipped back in again.

"Now get ready, we're going back in time."

"How far?"

"As far as we need to to get to the point before this black hole started, then we can have a look at the hidden planet and make a few adjustments to it." Steeleye took the small time-travel box from his belt and pressed the control that would speed them back.

"Now. Have a look out of the porthole, see if you can see any change."

"Jees, you said it. There's a bloody great star out there."

"Any planetary bodies?"

"Can't see for the light."

"Wait, let's see if the monitor on this thing can shade the light out and give us a better view." Steeleye turned the monitor screen on and adjusted filters across it.

"There we are, that's it. The only planet within reach of the star, that's the one. Come, we'll get a bit closer and see who's living there."

"Won't he see us?"

"Sure, but we shall do a bit of bluffing. You just keep quiet, leave the chat to me."

"Anything you say, chief."

They cruised into orbit and hailed the planet on the sub-space frequencies.

"We are in distress and need help, please respond."

No reply.

"He's on the loo."

"Shh. We are in distress and need help. If you can allow us landing we will not trouble you and will depart immediately repair has been completed. Please respond."

"Landing clear, set down under these co-ordinates."

The reply was steady and unconcerned. Steeleye set the co-ordinates and commenced landing, the motors coughing a little as they came down.

"Now remember, not a word, play mute or something."

"Oh that shouldn't be too difficult, I am quiet by nature, as you know."

Steeleye gave Vandal a sidelong look and he grinned sheepishly.

Landing completed, Steeleye opened the exit hatches and descended, his eye ready for danger.

"You are welcome to my planet, please be my guests." Steeleye had altered his physique slightly, making himself shorter and more average in appearance. However, his steel eye belied this apparent normality.

"What the . . . " Vandal turned to see the change in his friend's shape and stifled a screech of surprise.

"Are you hurt either of you? Do you need medical aid?"

The Calvanese occupant of the planet was humanoid, his head large and his neck muscles sturdy. However, his shoulders were very narrow and his twelve fingers webbed. His face was expressionless and mask-like. There was no smile to greet them but he used his hands as though they were his prime means of expression, vividly accenting his words with the emotion his face lacked. His hands spread a smile and Vandal felt almost safe on this strange hidden world.

"We are grateful to you for your welcome and we need only rest for ourselves and some repair work on the craft. May I introduce my colleague and engineer, his name is Vandal, mine is Steeleye."

"Welcome again, Vandal and Steeleye, please be free to stay with me as long as you need."

They were led from the landing area into the body of the great house.

"You have a fine home, we are fortunate to be here."

"I live happily, alone. There are no problems and I spend as much time here as I can. My home planet is Calve, some distance away. Come I will show you your rooms."

They were taken to two large rooms in the upper part of the house where all facilities appeared ready for any unexpected guests.

The room designated to Steeleye was old-fashioned but pleasing, with electric lighting and hot water on tap.

"Wow, what a place." Steeleye heard Vandal exclaim as he was installed in the room next door.

"Take to your bed now. I will wake you when I need help. It will be after nightfall." They met briefly in the corridor and parted again to return to their rooms.

Steeleye sat on his bed, his head resting in his hands, his elbows on his knees, casting about him for a scheme that would catch the Sideways Man out in his time.

As he pondered, a thick line slanted into the room. Steeleye leapt to his feet, ready to face his enemy once again but it was Tousle who quivered into shape.

"You are recovered." Steeleye was filled with relief.

"I took advantage of time travel, Steeleye. It was nearly three weeks of electronic surgery for complete recovery, but I jumped a few times to be here and help you should you need it."

"I might. Have you come straight from Zrost?"

"Not quite, but Chaos sends her love to you."

"Good, I'm glad she is safe." As he spoke he wished he was there too.

"She wanted to come with me but I thought she would be more use to you in safety."

"You say you have come via some other place?"

"Yes. I spent a few days in the castle on the Crystal Planet and I think I have solved the Tetrahecular. There is a way into that crossword box without the answers to the questions. All we need in fact is to get Kimber there."

"What, into the castle?"

"Into the room of the crossword. That room is a connection with the Tetrahecular and only Kimber's presence in it will release the rights of freeway in the Wideways to his successor. He has outlived his term."

"Term?"

"Yes. That is why he has not returned there. He could have killed or banished Yellow long before and repossessed the castle but he dared not enter the castle for more than the briefest visit for the Tetrahecular would have withdrawn his power. No one can hold it for more than 1,000 years."

"And Kimber has for 7,000."

"Yes. He is a wanted man. Wanted by the Tetrahecular which claims back its right to bestow the powers on the next claimant."

"How did you find all this out?"

"Yellow's notes. He kept extensive records of his time in the castle. He had plenty of time after all. And amongst them is the interpretation of the mathematical magic symbol."

"So, we must inveigle Kimber back to his home. But how?"

"There must be a way." Tousle set his mind to work.

Steeleye stood and switched on his X-ray beams to search the house.

"Hey, look at this, there's a cavity under the house. A basement of some kind. Perhaps we could do something down there."

"Come, we'll go down and see."

They descended into the basement and began their insurance for the future.

"I have prepared a meal for you. Perhaps if you have rested well enough now you would like to partake of it with me." The Calvanese occupant of the hidden planet knocked gently on Steeleye's door. There was silence from within.

"Heavy sleeper. Steeleye, a meal is prepared for you and your friend, you would be most welcome at my table." Still absolute silence. He tried the door and it opened immediately.

"Gone!" He made his way through the house and searched every room, a blaster held close to his tunic, but there was no sign of anyone within or out.

"Strange, their craft is still here, how could they have left?"

Beyond the day that the builder of the house was gone, beyond the slip of the planet into the black hole, Kimber sat calmly in the same house, alone but for his wandering ghost who walked his habitual way – to the distress of the robot hiding in the broom cupboard.

In the bedroom stood three unexpected guests who had outsayed their welcome for near on fifty thousand years.

Kimber had grown accustomed to these appearances of the old owner of the house, and had not tampered with the projector for he felt strangely consoled by the old ghost's presence. However, he no longer watched it walk, he knew by habit exactly when it would pass his door and go on down to the other end of the verandah. He did not even look up as out of the corner of his eye he saw it move between the door posts. But he did look up when he realised that it had stopped and was standing still in the doorway staring at him.

He blinked, but, long accustomed to emergencies, stood up and levelled the small hand blaster he kept constantly beside him. The phantom did not move.

Kimber waited, wondering whether, in a moment of doubt, it might simply have made a mistake and taken the wrong turn and perhaps would soon turn round and leave him his privacy. But of course this was quite illogical and the apparition was still there. Then he noticed that there appeared to be something else behind it.

Another, much taller figure, filling the whole doorway.

"Who is it?" he ordered, but there was no response.

The ghost suddenly turned its head round as though trying to see who stood behind him. As he did so the figure raised his hands and the ghost vanished. An image of Steeleye stood in the doorway.

Kimber instantaneously blasted to the heart of his towering foe but to no effect. He stood his ground.

"Playing ghost-hunting, Kimber?"

"How did you find me?"

"No matter, I am here. And I am here to take from you what is not your right to keep, Kimber."

"So, you have been tampering with the Tetrahecular. I wondered when you would fathom it out."

"Perhaps you would be kind enough to hand over the Wideways Rights to their next owner."

"Ha, ha, so you have your eye on the Wideways now eh, now that Yellow is gone to his makers." Kimber stood before the image of his enemy.

"Well, Steeleye, you'll have to chase me if you want it, and you may find my skill through the Wideways distracting."

"I find your skill as a booby-trapper irritating."

"Why don't you appear in the flesh, instead of this insubstantial charade. How did you get at my resident ghost?"

"Simple enough, just a parlour trick, Kimber."

"So you have not meddled with his control centre?"

"What control centre?"

"Ha, good, then now we shall have some fun. Goodbye, Steeleye. Follow if you can." Kimber turned and was gone. But Steeleye and Tousle and Vandal were ready this time and turned sidelong with Kimber into the Wideways.

Kimber had set a scene for the three intrepid pursuers. As they all turned back into the time dimensions the expected changes from one world to another in endless sequence did not occur.

Instead, they stood, side by side looking out over an endless plain. There seemed no horizon; land going on forever and never joining the sky.

On the surface of this barren plateau were small, dotted areas of life-like towns seen from a high-flying craft at night, their tiny sequinned lights, shining evidence of intelligence. There was no order to their placing and no roads or tracks joined them together but around the whole was a straight line of mountains forming a square like a game board.

"He's making it easy for us." Tousle spoke almost in a whisper. The landscape was covered in a soft mist that was settled within the border of the finely chiselled mountains. It floated smoothly as a blanket of liquid oxygen over the three large areas of light and the many smaller ones.

"What is it?" Steeleye asked.

"A visual manifestation; Kimber is displaying his powers again." They watched over the strange naturally walled valley like travellers preparing to enter a new world, uncertain of their route. Beyond the mountain ranges, on the far distant side, there was nothing, and to either side also, nothing. There was no opportunity for uncertainty, for their direction was set for them; they would have to enter the first small "town" and see what Kimber had laid for them.

"Sitting targets, all three of you." Steeleye, Tousle and Vandal ducked down, still jittery from their experiences in the chase.

"Where is he?" Vandal hissed out a comical whisper, avoiding any attempt to look for himself.

"Down there." Tousle whispered also and then grunted at his own apeing. "Down there on the mountain."

"What's he doing?" Vandal continued to whisper like a frightened cowboy behind a rock waiting to be shot at.

"Stop whispering, you numbskull, if he wants to hear you, he can. Just wait and see." Tousle was irritated by their defensive position. He felt foolish.

"Cease your chatter, idiots. You are unworthy of the chase. Nevertheless I have created a platform to play our game upon. We are all chess pieces on a board. You will chase and you will see that I will manoeuvre your every move." Kimber's voice suddenly boomed across the air vibrating with his fury. "For hear this, Steeleye, I am the Lord of the Wideways. This, that you see before you, is my domain, and you will suffer for your trespass into a world you do not comprehend." Kimber paused, his thin shrivelled body twisting slightly in the billowing mist which reached up like many hands from the valley to grasp at his legs and skinny trunk. "Come now, follow me into the landscape of the Wideways and see the times turn, the sideways worlds that I know so well."

Kimber sped down the mountainside growing smaller with the distance, scampering like a mountain goat until he reached the level ground and at once was lost into the heart of the first city.

"Is this one world or three?" Steeleye asked Tousle turning for a moment from his devil's viewpoint.

"This is three totally separate worlds, Steeleye, plucked by Kimber from their proper place in time and positioned on a podium for us to wonder at his ingenuity."

"He's been at it a while, though, I mean, I could be that good if I'd been around for 7,000 years." Vandal was bemused by the sights of such fantasy, still trying to keep a hold on the comedy of the situation.

"Well, we had better begin. We have a long way to go." They moved down into the valley and entered the first world.

"This is London." Tousle estimated. "Mid-1970s, but not the London we know from our past. A new London."

A row of tall houses stood before them, built in Victorian times, either side of a road filled with milling people, loading large cases and personal possessions from the houses into various vehicles in the street. The three moved between the people all of whom looked tense and frightened, some were crying and everywhere was an atmosphere of panic.

"What game is this?" Steeleye felt the surrounding danger, unable to make sense of a situation which did not tally with any history tape he had seen.

"This is not an Earth that I have ever watched on the Time Viewers. We are in the mid-1970s in London but no such panic was ever in this place at this time." Tousle searched for a reference point to establish a strain of logic in his organised brain.

The people were frantic, moving like ants. They were attempting to satisfy a desire for order but their fear engendered only a grasp at survival. Tousle watched, unseen, for everyone was so involved with flight that his presence remained unnoticed despite his size and unique appearance.

One family unit nearby with two very small children epitomised the state of all those around them. The man was tall, blond-haired, beside a woman, the mother of the two children, her dark hair hung loose about her shoulders, a blonde child cradled against her side. The father carried a boy no more than four earth years of age and crying; not from pain but a knowledge of his parent's confusion and concern, his own sense of vulnerability.

They burst out of the house with bags and hastily tied parcels.

A wild dishevelled man rushed after them brandishing a long-barrelled rifle. He put the weapon to his shoulder and aimed at the man as he dashed down the stair. The gun went off but the kick was so great that the missile from the barrel swished past the father's head, missing him by only a matter of centimetres. It thudded into an unsuspecting woman trying desperately to drag a small boy into a large vehicle on the other side of the road. She died instantly, and Tousle watched the father's reaction.

Though the woman was not known to him, his temper turned in a split second as he saw the woman killed, from fear and anguish into a fury of desperate anger. The most murderous glare spread across his tired face. The woman's body had snapped like a broken twig, crumpling to the ground leaving her child in bewilderment and unknowing horror. The man's wife tried to drag him back but he thrust his screaming son into her clutching hands and bounded back up the stair to grasp the rifleman about the chest. The fellow was not small, indeed no smaller than his aggressor who nevertheless plucked him from the ground, lifting his entire body high into the air. He held him there for no more than a moment as he turned and looked straight at Steeleye. He saw him, disconcerted by his unfamiliar appearance, his own face dazed, doubting. A frown spread across it as he prepared to dash the man to the ground. A frown that uttered a dreaming doubt; a look that said he would not believe any of the events that surrounded him; neither the war that was raging nor the murder he was about to commit. A face that expressed his own turmoil at a sudden change from normal human behaviour into that of a killer. Steeleye's strange and piercing visage now only merged into his crazed state and he instantly dismissed it, casting the fellow from the stair-well onto the basement stone where his body snapped, kicked and died.

Across the road a woman was being attacked and another stabbed over and over again as she tried to prevent a man from leaving her house with food and valuable goods. Her husband was already dead, his head split open.

Steeleye picked up a newspaper from the ground and read the headline to Tousle and Vandal:

"War is declared. World War Two begins."

"World War Two, it's a printing error," Vandal suggested, not really believing it.

"Don't be ridiculous, this *is* World War Two, but thirty years later than on the Earth we know. We must be thousands of dimensions removed from old Earth. They've only just reached that point old Earth reached now." Steeleye looked at the houses, as the people left the street in droves.

The three travellers entered one of the abandoned homes to try and find some evidence to show why war had broken out now, after so lengthy a peace.

The inside of the ground floor was ransacked, clothes and pictures, mirrors, letters, all manner of personal possessions were scattered across the floor. The bed was turned back as though its occupants had been sleeping when the panic started. But why such a panic, war doesn't develop that suddenly, the newspaper was today's date, what was the hurry?

"Here, look, another report." Vandal read from a magazine thrown into the corner.

"The United States of Europe today declared open warfare upon the British Commonwealth of Nations." Something wrong there. "After a breakdown at the Watchforth talks over the use of Germ Bombs, General Gaston Bonvalet, leader of the U.S.E. forces declared his intention to mobilise air forces in an immediate attack upon London, to display the levels of power against which the British Commonwealth risked setting itself. General Bonvalet said that he would expect this attack to be treated as an example of the power in the hands of the U.S.E. and that it would hopefully end any further violence. He would hope that the suffering inflicted upon London would act as a warning."

"Some warning." Vandal threw the paper down. "No wonder they're panicking." As he spoke there was a thunderous shaking in the house. The windows rattled, the walls shook and the lights went out.

Suddenly, outside it was night. The magazine Vandal had been reading sailed through the air out of the room and vanished. The bed, unmade when they walked in, swept back its sheets and covered two bodies that had appeared without warning and now lay in deep slumber. The broken windows were whole again, the hastily packed cases were empty and back inside a cupboard. Like a witches' feast night everything happened in reverse before their dumb-struck faces.

The door of the cupboard opened, the case full of scattered clothes unloaded itself into drawers that opened and shut like a series of hungry mouths. The empty case closed and sped into the cupboard and the door closed. Then all was silent.

"Get into the Wideway Alley. We must watch this, I think we're about to see the whole thing enacted over again."

"For chrissakes why?" Vandal followed them out of sight.

"Don't ask me, another of Kimber's games."

As they watched, one of the sleepers shifted restlessly in his bed, turned over and sat up on the side. He was unable to sleep, got up and went to the kitchen to make something to eat. In the middle of cutting a sandwich he stopped and turned his head as though he detected something. After another few moments he stopped again and walked back into the bedroom. Something in his mind had made him decide to call someone on the telephone for he picked up the receiver and dialled, carrying the telephone as he did so out of the bedroom area and back into the kitchen on the long lead. He finished dialling and waited for a reply.

"Eric? Yes, I'm sorry, I had to call you . . . Yes I know it's late but I had to call . . . Listen, I got a funny feeling, something's wrong isn't it?" The man shifted onto the high stool that stood by the kitchen table. "Don't Eric, I know something's wrong, I just have this feeling that the talks have gone wrong . . . don't play riddles with me, you know very well what talks. Yes. What is it, what are they going to do?" He paused and as he listened his face went grey. As though he had been told of his own death sentence his eyes clouded and his shoulders seemed to droop under the weight of what he was being told.

"Oh my God. Oh my God." he hesitated, dropping the receiver for a moment from his ear. But he gathered himself and put it back again. "How much time?" Another pause. "What should I do? I can't just leave everybody, I can't let them all die. I've got to warn them . . . What do you mean more deaths by panic? You can't just let people stay in their beds and be killed off by those bloody germ bombs. You've got to give them a chance. If we all stay here . . . No, I know I could get away, but what about all the others, Eric? I can't just leave them, there are hundreds . . . Yes, I know. No, I can't, damn you. I must tell them." He slammed the receiver down and walked to the bedroom, but stopped. He walked back and stopped again, not sure which way to turn in his fear. Finally he went to the cupboard and began to pull out the case that had only moments before travelled into it in its eerie fashion. He pulled open drawers and began to pack clothes. Then his wife woke up.

"What is it, John? What's going on?"

"You've got to get up, quickly." John went to her bedside, ready to calm her.

"What is it?" She jumped up, feeling his panic.

"They're going to bomb us." As he spoke the words there was another shake, another rumble in the room. The windows crashed out of their frames and the plaster began to fall from the ceiling. The movements of both John and his wife were frozen, not through any sense of fear but with a solidity as if they were statues. Their features still set in the same frightful visage as when the jump took place.

They were quite still. The pieces of shattered window hung in the air as though they hesitated to fall. The three in the Wideway Alley were thrust out of it, kicked like drunks discharged from a bar. They looked about them in the room, Vandal's eyes wide with fear, no foolery now, he was genuinely scared. There was a gentle rumbling that came from outside and built up around the three as they stood in the room. The two humans sat, still frozen into no time, unaffected by the time breakdown.

Then without further warning Steeleye found himself separated from his two friends, whirling through the air, head over heals in the most uncontrollable fashion. He thought, for thought was the only slow thing left in his world of sudden chaos. Thought could be slow, it could be controlled, monitored, like nothing else now for he realised that the infrastructure of time and matter was finally breaking down. Kimber's plans to centralise the Wideways of time into one world were failing right around them. He thought in that second and willed that he should bring his own body down safely somewhere. He centred his thoughts on that one intention and somehow succeeded, landing with a dull thump on a piece of ground.

A large truck sailed over his head, its appearance far in advance of the world he had just left, with atomic powered engines. It hit the air, nothing solid prevented it, but a barrier of some kind had halted its progress and it erupted into flames, exploding with a crash that made all other explosions merely breaking eggs. The blast echoed through the air repeating itself through several times. A colossal wind roared about his ears so that he could barely turn his head to look about him, forcing his breath from his lungs and putting him in doubt of the completeness of his body. Steeleye reassured himself that every limb was in place and attempted to stand.

"What a mess," he muttered as he fell to the ground again, unable to brace against the wind. He looked up to where the sky should have been and it was as though there was a mirror image of where he sat, in the air. Another Earth flew overhead, sailing past like a planet out of orbit. After it came a series of changing worlds, each one, though similar, was slowly differing from the last; some on fire, some carrying huddled people, clutching one another on the thin blasted ground.

"Hi." Vandal landed beside Steeleye from nowhere. "Where've you been? I was looking for you."

"Right here, what about you, and where's Tousle?" Steeleye again tried to stand and this time succeeded, his hair flowing round his head.

"No idea, he went off like you did and left me to fend for myself. What's happening? Any idea?"

"I think the whole time structure's broken down. I reckon Kimber has lost control."

"Boy oh boy, that's going to be fun."

Vandal did not attempt any increase in his height from the ground. He simply clutched the grass where he sat, holding on. There was nothing in place. The thick mist of dust that was blown along before the gusting wind obscured much and only tumbling masses of earth and ruins from several unconnected worlds seemed visible beyond it. There were no houses, no trees or people, nothing familiar now. Only a wilderness of flying debris, that floated unceremoniously on the rising air into a storm of chaos. Nearby stood the remains of a shattered space craft from another world. It glowed red, burning up from inside, its hull splintered and battered from being smashed against the hard ground. It shivered like a small toy, its bulk negated by the force of the time storm. What had once been a bridge was now a mass of twisted girders, rising from the ground like a monster from the deep of a lake. It rose up in the reverse of a sinking ship, levelled itself into the air and collapsed onto the ground, then disappeared completely from sight. There was no sense or logic left; everything had been forced into isolation and fended alone without the protection of order. Chaos as a natural state had returned to the Universe, and if someone or something didn't put a stop to it soon then everything would collapse completely.

Still clutching the earth, Steeleye and Vandal tried to make some sense out of their surroundings.

"Over there, look, it's Kimber." Vandal finally managed to stand but sat down again sharply as Steeleye pointed out the Sideways Man.

"What the hell's he doing now?"

Kimber was standing stock still, his hands raised high into the air as though he summoned some power.

They couldn't hear what he said but faint words drifted through the air and Kimber waved his hands, like a magician casting spells.

Steeleye and Vandal looked up at the drifting sky. As

they watched two very bright stars appeared in the heavens and began rushing towards them. They were many thousands of kilometres apart but charging through the sky, massing down upon them. As they came closer and the heat turned to a colossal burning intensity they stopped. Right there in the sky they seemed to stand still, held there by some time power wielded by Kimber.

Then he shook like a man possessed and waved his hands again at the sky. From nowhere came a massive meteorite, speeding across the sky directly towards the suns.

"It's the energy crash." Steeleye spluttered the words.

"The what?" Vandal was nowhere near understanding.

"The energy crash, the one that Kimber used to power the castle's time warps on the Crystal Planet. He's brought it here, he changed time and space to bring that energy here, right to this place."

"Why?"

"I don't know, I don't know, but I fear it. I think he's going to destroy Time, he's going to disrupt the infrastructure of the Universe using that collision as an energy source . . . if we don't stop him."

Steeleye was right. The Sideways Man had once discovered the collision between two stars and a huge meteorite. He had tapped that energy to power his time chamber in the castle and now he was dragging it from its correct time to use it against the Universe of the Wideways and destroy everything.

Tousle appeared beside them. He moved with them closer to Kimber.

"Come, Steeleye, turn into the Wideways. Make your line, make a bow." Steeleye obeyed and Vandal watched the two powerful creatures. Steeleye became a thick pliant line in the air and Tousle did the same. The first line curved smoothly into the shape of an archer's bow and the second slid like a long straight arrow onto the string. The arrow drew back against the tension of the bow and as it did so Kimber looked towards them.

"Jiminy Cricket, get on with it, he's seen you." For that instant Kimber lost his control on the stars and they vanished back into their own time. The arrow pulled right back and Tousle sped through the air fast as light itself. The point struck clean home, sinking deep into Kimber's chest and withdrawing immediately leaving a huge hole. Kimber screeched at the air, cursed like a mighty monster, flashing his evil eyes at his challengers and took a blaster from his belt. He raised it but Steeleye was faster. He opened the aperture of his eye full and blasted at Kimber with a furious heat. Kimber fell back, crashing to the ground. The world around them was still in chaos but the private battle in this place was uninterrupted.

Kimber was gushing blood from his chest wound and howling in pain. He grasped the ground where he lay and bellowed at Steeleye to leave him.

"I will have your powers, Kimber. You have kept them too long. Now you hope to destroy everything in your jealousy, but I will not allow it. I will be the Sideways Man, for your term is complete. Come with me to the Crystal Planet and we can settle up with the Tetrahecular."

"I will not fight you more, Steeleye, you have beaten me, but be merciful. Help me, for my wounds are fatal, and if I die the powers of the Wideways will die too. Then you will have nothing." Steeleye hesitated as he stood before Kimber and in that instant the Sideways Man lifted his feet and kicked Steeleye sharply in the stomach thrusting him backwards onto the ground.

"Fool," the Sideways Man shouted, drawing the blaster back again and closing the contact. Steeleye rolled and the earth where he had lain was sheared up and disrupted by the beam.

"You will die for your foolishness." Kimber fired again but was hampered by his wound and his aim went wide of the mark. Steeleye turned his head, his eye glowing with fury, for Kimber had played with him once again.

"Now you will see the full fury of the Eumig eye." He fired a dreadful blast at Kimber's body and blasted away both the blaster and the arm that carried it. Kimber screeched an echoing scream that reverberated across a million times. Grasping the stump of his arm he stood before Steeleye and staggered back. Steeleye turned the eye upon him once more, a full wide aperture of heat that crippled the senses, bowing his body to kneeling before the mighty giant. He could not think for the agony of the blast incensing his entire body and mind, preventing him from any defensive move.

Steeleye continued the blast in his anger, managing only just to prevent himself from reducing Kimber to a burnt cinder. He approached, still firing until he stood over Kimber's inert body, then he increased the blast and rendered him unconcious.

Kimber fell to the ground with a dull thud, rolling over, he lay on his back.

But as Steeleye and now Tousle and Vandal watched, the body faded, slowly losing its substance, and soon vanished completely, leaving the marks of the falling force but nothing more.

"God be a witness," Steeleye screamed at the air. "He has escaped again."

"No, he has some automatic device that takes him back to his hideaway planet. He will go into the trap we have set for him. Come, we must return to the castle and await his arrival."

Chapter 16

Kimber staggered across the grounds of his hideaway planet and touched the stone below the house. It opened and he fell in, crashing onto the floor, rolling towards the place his predecessors had told him would take him finally to oblivion. This was the time to go, and he would go taking the Wideways with him.

He touched the floor plate that controlled the ghost and the 4D box in the centre of the room. A wall opened to one side. It slid back revealing a twisting cloud of vapour.

"The last to walk through that door was the builder of this place. Now I shall follow him and find eternity." He stepped into the cavity and the very moment he was past the wall he was grasped with such strength that he could not move or resist. His body was strapped tight in a strait-jacket of force. He was whisked through time and space on a journey he tried to assure himself would lead at last to a land of forever, where he would be free of his attackers and left alone, without life or death, still cradling his powers.

But the Sideways Man soon ended his dream for within no time of his departure his body was thrown violently to a solid earth where it rolled semi-conscious to turn and look up at the two creatures he thought he had escaped. Once again he was in the castle on the Crystal Planet and standing over him were Steeleye and Tousle.

"We have been expecting you, Kimber, for this is the place where you were bound to come by the powers of mathematics and magic."

Kimber, ever determined against defeat, managed to stand, shaking on his weak feet, the stump of his arm bleeding still. He staggered forward towards them both and then, without warning, became still. His body changed from a broken, battered effigy of Kimber into a solid erect figure, hazed by a surrounding light of translucence. His figure became whole. His hand was there again, undamaged. The wounds were healed and he stood like an angel of light, rounded about with strength and power. A voice sounded in the chamber.

"Kimber, you have misused your granted powers. Your greed has taken you into damaging ways, inappropriate to the Master of the Wideways. The Tetrahecular gives strength and knowledge of complete time only to those it chooses and will grant that to no one for more than an equal time. Your predecessors were never guilty of such deception and the chase for recovery of the right has now been completed. Your powers are gone. But no creature can hold the Wideways in its grasp and be punished thereafter. Thus the Tetrahecular grants you a stay of execution but banishes you to the realms you so desire, those of eternity. You shall live and die for ever in the lands of nowhere. You shall not suffer more for your crime against infinity, but you shall be gone now to dwell amongst the living dead who have gone before you."

The silence was filled with a strange cry and Kimber dissolved into the air.

A soft speaking wind shifted through the chamber where they stood. In the room with the crossword box and in the presence of the Tetrahecular they watched as the walls of the castle vanished. Before them was a whole world where once there had been the sides of a small room.

The musical wind mingled with the air about them and sent small shivers down their backs. In front of their eyes they observed the story of their chase. There was Yellow standing in welcome at the door of the castle, they saw the brilliant colours of the "Ifinasis" as its lights streamed from the body of the Crystal Planet. Before them was the famous auction when Yellow first brought the wrath of the Sideways Man upon him; Boy disappearing into the time chamber and Steeleye fighting the strange weapons that Kimber set against him. Then the beginning of the chase that took them through every time and many places, to

Tan-Minor and Chaos's first meeting with Vandal, to Gyp and the vagrants; they saw Carosh through Vandal's eyes, Steeleye's death through Chaos's, and the meeting of the Eumigs again after so long. They watched the battle between Steeleye and the Codas and the fateful death of Yellow who stood as though alive before them in the image of the misty plain that spread at their feet. They saw it all. Kimber's hideaway, the home-made ghost, and the awful chase, wars on crazy unknown Earths and the final breakdown of the time infrastructure.

But now they were at the end, in the hands of the Tetrahecular. The picture faded before them and there lay in its place an empty plain, quite devoid of life or death. And the Tetrahecular spoke.

"The Kimbernium is gone. The powers of the Wideways must now be reallocated and it is possible that one who stands at the foot of infinity would wish to succeed. But first you must examine what powers you hope to aspire to. Do not imagine that because you have used the Wideways you know what is there. The powers that rested so heavily upon Kimber's shoulders are far greater than you can hitherto have imagined for in your hands during the next thousand years will sit the giving of life or the awarding of death. Each Sideways Man is greater than the one before him. Now Steeleye, step forward, for in this way of time and life you will be given the chance to say no."

Before them materialized a small hut. It measured some three metres in height and could have bulked no more than five wide.

"The journey is for one who would stand eligible for the power of the Wideways – only Steeleye may enter." The voice of the Tetrahecular gave Tousle grief and Vandal relief. Steeleye stepped forward, ducked his head to enter the open door and walked into an unknown world.

Around the outside was the tingling aura of time and then blackness. As Steeleye entered, the aura about the battered old hut changed to many colours as though it reflected its new occupant. Tousle and Vandal saw Steeleye enter and immediately saw him walk out again, as though he had walked through the door and with hardly the time to turn round came back. That is what *they* say – but within that second of their time Steeleye saw much more.

Upon entry Steeleye's first glance settled on a huge glass prism which stood in empty space and through it was thrown a time stream. On its other side were millions of worlds, in shafts of time, spread out in perfect formation, each line a world with its alternatives. Steeleye walked forward, passing through the prism's centre and watched his own body duplicate in the infinite stream as it had done in the castle's Wideway chamber.

Once on the other side he was no longer in space but slowly, like a gentle, gradual suggestion, a road spread out before him. Tentatively the surrounding landscape came into focus. It was twilight, a time when the day can be forgotten.

Steeleye walked the road, swept by the wind that buffeted his face – the air gave him the comfort and security he had not felt during the whole of his recent ordeals. There was a feeling that all was well with the worlds.

On either side were tall trees which swayed in the gusting wind as slowly the night settled about him. The road soon turned and forked, bearing left and right before him. Standing at the point of that fork stood a tall impressive man. As Steeleye walked closer he saw that the man had no face – his head was clean shaven and featureless, light haloes about every curve and a clear silken cloak covered his body. The wind shifted and circled them as they faced one another, leaves blowing around his feet.

Fluttering in a whirlwind the leaves began to spiral upwards, outlining his sculptured shape. The magic billowing wind altered its contours at each level, turning the cloak into a pair of generous white trousers. Swirling up past his waist and blowing the top into a white, loose coat with large shining buttons upon it.

It began then to explore his head, gusting the leaves in the continuing circle. In the half-light it wreathed him with long golden tresses, and upon his empty face fashioned a wide mouth, long nose and two large eyes with ovoid, golden, shining pupils.

The leaves drew back, having crowned his head momentarily, and flurried into nothingness. Steeleye looked – but could barely utter the name that rounded on his tongue. As he spoke finally, the wind brought rain dense and slanting. The figure before him glowed against the dark and yet was not wet.

Steeleye smiled the name, "Yellow."

And the rain beat about his face, drenching his entire body, strangely humbled, as he stared in wonder at the old Pierrot who had never died.

"Steeleye, come. I am here to show you through the Wideways – for I am the Tetrahecular."

"You knew what would happen – in all that time in the castle you knew what the future held."

"Yes – I knew. Now come, you must choose the road you will take. One will give you nothing and return you to your family on Zrost, the other will take you back into the castle where Tousle and Vandal wait to join you and that road will reward your past endeavours with the prize of the Wideways. Which will you take, Steeleye? Which will you take?"

Tousle smiled, Vandal laughed. "Wow, that was quick."